MW00884638

WHEN GIANTS BURN

Also by
BETH VRABEL

To Tell You the Truth
Lies I Tell Myself

BETH VRABEL

WHEN GIANTS BURN

Atheneum Books for Young Readers
New York London Toronto Sydney New Delhi

atheneum

ATHENEUM BOOKS FOR YOUNG READERS

An imprint of Simon & Schuster Children's Publishing Division

1230 Avenue of the Americas, New York, New York 10020

ATHENEUM BOOKS FOR YOUNG READERS is a registered trademark of Simon & Schuster, Inc. Atheneum logo is a trademark of Simon & Schuster, Inc.

For information about special discounts for bulk purchases, please contact Simon & Schuster Special Sales at 1-866-506-1949 or business@simonandschuster.com.

The Simon & Schuster Speakers Bureau can bring authors to your live event. For more information or to book an event, contact the Simon & Schuster Speakers Bureau at 1-866-248-3049 or visit our website at www.simonspeakers.com.

Interior design by Irene Metaxatos

The text for this book was set in Adobe Caslon Pro.

Manufactured in the United States of America

0523 FFG

First Edition

10 9 8 7 6 5 4 3 2 1

Library of Congress Cataloging-in-Publication Data

Names: Vrabel, Beth, author. • Title: When giants burn / Beth Vrabel. • Description: First edition. | New York : Atheneum Books for Young Readers, 2023. | Audience: Ages 8-12. | Audience: Grades 4-6. | Summary: Wanting to escape his family life, sixth grader Hayes flies off with his misfit friend Gerty to protect a clonal colony of aspen from a wildfire, but the two quickly realize the importance of everything they tried to leave behind. • Identifiers: LCCN 2022019356 (print) | LCCN 2022019357 (ebook) | ISBN 9781665918626 (hardcover) | ISBN 9781665918633 (ebook) • Subjects: CYAC: Friendship—Fiction. | Family life—Fiction. | Wildfires—Fiction. | Survival—Fiction. | Aspen—Fiction. | Trees—Fiction. | LCGFT: Novels. Classification: LCC PZ7.V9838 Wh 2023 (print) | LCC PZ7.V9838 (ebook) | DDC [Fic]—dc23 • LC record available at https://lccn.loc.gov/2022019356 • LC ebook record available at https://lccn.loc.gov/2022019357

To twelve-year-old Beth.
Can you believe it?

WHEN GIANTS BURN

GERTY

A high, keening sound rocks through me. Hayes. He's screaming, his mouth an open cave. And the side of the mountain is where the sky ought to be.

Yet my voice is steady when I shout, "Hold on!"

His arms wrap around my waist. I cover his hands with mine as everything I built shatters around us.

The ground is so hard, and I am too soft.

1

GERTY

Ten days earlier

Hearing about other people's dreams is boring, but Jennifer says I need friends and that, since she's my mom, I have to listen to her. Which, being honest, is confusing because Jennifer and Alex also say their goal is to raise entirely independent children. Yet here I am, being forced to listen to Hayes Teller's boring dream.

I try to tune him out. Alex, my dad, says it's important to take stock of every room, figure out two modes of exit. Obviously, the door behind me counts as one way to leave the guidance counselor's office. But I could scale the bookcase easy, kick out the window, and drop to the ground in a loose roll. If I had to, I mean.

"It's a fire," Hayes says. This gets my attention. I know

a lot about fires. "But big, wide, so it's like the ocean." His voice trips over the word *ocean*. "And, like, I'm running toward it, okay? I'm running toward it, but it keeps getting farther away. No matter how fast I run, it's the same distance away."

Mrs. Freid, the guidance counselor, is supposed to be leading this discussion, but she's staring into space like it's the romance novel she has next to the lunch box at the edge of her desk.

"Fire doesn't go back," I say. "It swoops forward." Hayes raises an eyebrow at me. He has thick slashes for eyebrows. I like that about him. "Wildfire does *sound* like an ocean, though. My dad showed me a video of when they set thousands of Fishlake Forest acres on fire—a controlled burn. It sounded like the ocean. I mean, what I think the ocean is like. I've never seen one."

Hayes flinches. He doesn't like to talk about fire, even though he brought it up. He keeps a lot of his words inside.

Me? Words spurt out of my mouth. Especially when it's stuff I know a lot about and think other people ought to know. I dip my voice lower, leaning in to Hayes a little so Mrs. Freid won't hear and start in on her "wait for social cues" lecture. (Apparently, not everyone wants to share in my knowledge all the time. Sometimes, according to Mrs. Freid, they simply want to "be heard.") "Safest place in a wildfire, generally speaking, is to get behind the flames—where the ground's already been burned to a crisp, so nothing's left to reignite. But it's probably a good idea to get a fire dome. Compact foil. They reflect the heat, but they cost, like, four hundred dollars."

Mrs. Freid snaps back to focus. She blinks a couple of times. Her head tilts to the side. If a thought bubble bloomed over Mrs. Freid's head during our "group sessions," most of the time it would read, *What is wrong with these kids?* Or maybe, *How did I get here?*

"Here" is Rabbit, Utah, where I've lived for the past six years and where my mom grew up. It's a town of fewer than two thousand people, and a school district with fewer than a hundred students and one glamorous-looking professional counselor from New York. She's in over her head. My dad taught me how to look for the signs of panic in people and animals.

While I've lived in Rabbit for more than half my life, last year was my first time out of homeschooling. My parents say it's necessary for me to understand why they chose to self-isolate and move from Salt Lake City after . . . well, when they did. They think middle school will be the thing that really solidifies within me a desire to leave the social fabric behind.

Mrs. Freid keeps asking me to think about *my* feelings during these sessions. How do *I* feel about being in school? Honestly, for the most part, I don't. Alex says people spend too much time thinking about their own feelings when they should be focused on two things only: today and tomorrow. Alex and Jennifer want me here, to learn as much about society and its meaninglessness as possible, so that's what I'm going to do.

But I guess if I had to admit it under torture, I'd say the cafeteria food is better than most of my family's cooking, gym class dodgeball beats fitness drills with Alex, and these sessions with Mrs. Freid allow me to put to good use lessons from *How to Analyze People: What CIA Spies Know but Hope You Never Will*. It's a book I've indefinitely borrowed from the town library. I'm good at most things, but my ability to read facial expressions is superior.

Hayes's biggest tells aren't on his face, though. They're in his hands. His hands clench a lot when he's nervous, and right now he can't seem to stop flexing them. But what did Mrs. Freid just say to trigger that response? I missed it. *Focus, Gerty.*

Since Hayes and I were both new last year, we got pulled into Mrs. Freid's office for twice-weekly lunch meetings. Hayes is also low on friendships (in society's dim view of socialization). He lives with his grandma and little brother, and I guess his mom now too. We just started sixth grade, and I thought Mrs. Freid visits would cut back this year, but I'm still here because of the whole scavenging thing that *some* people call stealing, even though they're wrong. And Hayes is still here because he doesn't have any friends.

Alex says survivors don't waste energy focusing on other people's woes. Even so, I know why Hayes and his brother, Charlie, moved in with old Doc Louise. Everyone in town does. It's because Hayes's mom was in prison back in California. She's out now and lives with them too.

Whereas I tend not to notice that other people don't want to hear about how to get out of dangerous situations, or about why their minds are closed to the reality of their insignificance in the vastness of nature, Hayes rarely talks about anything at all.

Aside from his eyebrows, I like one other thing about Hayes: in class, his head is always down on his desk. Being able to catch up on sleep regardless of conditions is an essential skill in crisis situations.

As I tune back in to the conversation, Mrs. Freid asks Hayes, "Could this nightmare have something to do with your mother?" I choke on a groan. Her dark eyes narrow at me. Mrs. Freid thinks everything wrong is because of our mothers. There's a picture of her with her own mother on her desk. The older Mrs. Freid looks like her daughter, only instead of smooth hair and tailored suits, she has hair braided in thick cornrows and loose clothing. They have the same smile, same straight white teeth, and same dark brown skin.

"You know, why am I still here?" Hayes says, and I wonder what's come over him today. "My mom's been out for three months. I thought when she was here in Rabbit too, I wouldn't have to come to these lunches anymore." He shoots a look my way. "No offense."

"None taken." I turn to Mrs. Freid. "Why *are* we here?" I know the answer, of course, but I want to hear her say it.

"The thing is," she begins, "you're both strange, unlikable children without any friends."

I'm joking. She doesn't say that. Really, Mrs. Freid says, "I think the three of us could use a safe place."

Her breathing is steady. She's looking Hayes in the eyes, her hands folded loosely and no fake smile on her face. All signs that she's being honest.

"Frankly speaking, Mrs. Freid," I say into the thick quiet that unfurls among us after her words, "the safest place is anywhere with me. I've studied jujitsu since I was a toddler. If things go sideways, I could break anyone's arm five different ways. Maybe more."

Mrs. Freid closes her eyes. The bell rings, and she startles. "Okay, this week's challenge: take a risk."

"Risks are not—"

She holds up a hand to cut off my words. "Not a physical risk. A social one. Do something with a friend, or a would-be friend. Let them know something about you."

It's a dirty, sneaky move to trick me like that. Mrs. Freid knows I can't back down from a dare.

So, on the bus ride home, I sit in front of Hayes's bench. I'm going to let him in on my secret. I figure it's safe to tell him, since he doesn't have any friends and I get the impression he doesn't talk to his mom or grandma all that much. At the last minute, though, I remember what my dad says: if you're going to do something, make sure it's worth your while. Efficiency is key to survival. "Want to come to my house? There's something I want to show you."

Hayes leans back on the sticky vinyl seat and closes his eyes as though running through a to-do list. "Yeah, I think I could make some time."

"Great. Meet me at the bus stop in an hour with a grocery cart."

Hayes's eyes pop open. "A grocery cart?"

I nod. "Or at least, two of its wheels."

"I don't . . . I don't have a grocery cart." Hayes's slashy eyebrows knit together.

I smirk. "Then get one."

Hayes glances behind him to Charlie, his little brother. Charlie's in fourth grade. He's sitting in the last row of the bus, talking to his friends. He has, like, six of them. That's a lot in Rabbit.

I'm glad my sister is too small to leave the house without Alex and Jennifer.

"Ooooohhh," says Jaxson, the jerk in the seat in front of me. "Hayes and Gerty, going on a date. You guys gonna go make out? You gonna—"

I lean forward so my forehead is about five inches from Jaxson's. I tilt my head to one side and then the other, eyes narrowed like a hawk's. Predators back down only to fiercer predators.

Jaxson faces forward again.

"Hey," Hayes says to me as we get off the bus. We both ignore Charlie calling out, "Where are you going, Hayes?"

"A grocery cart wheel?" Hayes asks me.

I hold up two fingers. "Two wheels. But to get them, you'd need a power drill, so maybe stick with the whole cart." I point to the ground. "Right here. One hour. If you're not back, I'll never talk to you again." Fine, I'll admit it, the way Hayes's mouth pops open and he jerks his head (signs of panic) is satisfying. He might not like me or want to be my friend, exactly, but we've been sitting at the same table in the cafeteria and hanging around near each other at recess. This confirms he'd rather be with me than totally alone. "I mean, I won't talk to you for a week, at least."

Hayes swallows. "Mrs. Freid did say to take a risk." He nods. "Where am I supposed—"

"Figure it out!" I say. "I promise, it'll be worth it." I lean in to him. "I'll show you my secret project."

"Your—"

"*Shh!*" I look around for eavesdroppers and spies. Seeing none except for Charlie, I poke Hayes in the chest. "One hour."

2

HAYES

Generally speaking, I'm not big on stealing stuff.

Yet when Gerty disappears into the woods at the edge of the bus stop, I stand there, thinking.

Grocery cart wheels? Is this some sort of test? Do I want to pass it?

Gerty's okay, I guess. I like being able to count on her saying something outrageous to shift the attention away from me with Mrs. Freid. I don't know for sure, but I think she does that on purpose. And knowing that she doesn't exactly keep her thoughts to herself makes me want to know what this secret is that she's keeping.

But is that worth this whole grocery cart wheel business?

I could simply go back to Grandma Louise's house and call Gerty's bluff. But Mom will be there, sitting at the kitchen table. She'll ask, "How was your day?" I'll have to listen to Charlie go on and on about how great his was, just awesome. Then she'll turn to me, and I'll have to either lie or tell her the truth. That it was awful. That I hated it. That I hate every day in Rabbit.

I turn toward town. I mean, I guess you could call it town. There's a gas station, a diner, a bar, and Quik Mart (which is so fast, it can't be bothered to use the *c*). All of them are about a half mile up the road.

"*Hayes!*" Charlie whines. "What am I supposed to tell Grandma Louise?"

"Tell her I'm with Gerty," I say, "and I'll be back by dark."

Charlie sighs and stomps off, kicking rocks.

Is it illegal to steal a grocery cart? I bet it is.

It's probably even worse to take the wheels off and leave a broken-down cart. That's probably two crimes.

This is all some sort of joke, so when I prove to Gerty . . . whatever it is that stealing a grocery cart proves . . . I'll wheel it back and no one will ever have to know.

My hands curl and open. Am I really going to do this?

The Quik Mart corrals are full of carts, but there are workers— bored-looking teenagers in yellow vests—coming in and out of the store to bring them back inside in long trains. I wish I had money. Then I'd fill up the cart with food and pretend my folks parked far away as I casually walked from the store.

Instead I'm here, stooped next to a big black cow, wondering if people get arrested for swiping grocery carts. I know, right? A cow. There are cows everywhere in Rabbit. The ranchers let them roam. They scared me at first, but I've been here long enough that they only really bother me when it snows. Then they crowd up the road, licking at the salt, and we have to start school late.

Once I'm arrested, I'll probably have to go to a group home. Charlie and me, we spent a night in one when Mom was arrested, before the social worker could get ahold of Grandma Louise. And then two more nights before she could get out to California. I don't want to talk about it.

I'd be whupped for sure if anyone in a group home found out I was there for stealing a grocery cart, of all things. Especially an empty one.

"Ah, come on!" One of the teenagers curses. A cart won't go into the train he's trying to make. He says another word I'm not allowed to say but think hard and often. He peels off the cart, shoving it to the side. "Ralph!" he shouts. The other teenager, nearly back into the store, doesn't turn around. "Ralph, take this one out back with all the other piece-of-[bad word here] carts!"

"Ha!" I gasp, startling the cow, which sidesteps away from me with a low moo. Whatever, judgmental cow.

This is my chance.

A few minutes later I'm stumbling through the parking lot of the diner across the street from Quik Mart, throwing my weight to the side every few feet to right the wonky cart

I'm liberating from the junk pile behind the store.

A tall, thin man, who looks too young for the scraggly mustache he's sporting, chuckles as he walks by. "If you're going to steal a cart, kid, shouldn't you at least get one that's full of groceries?" Something about his grin seems vaguely familiar.

The man opens the door to his beat-up sedan and slides in. I can see a pile of fast-food wrappers and crumpled clothes in the passenger seat. I'm about to explain that I'm not *stealing* the cart, since it was going to be junked anyway, when the door to the diner is thrown open and an older woman bellows, "Sparky! Get back in here and pay your bill!" She sprints out of the restaurant, her apron pockets jammed with napkins and straws.

The man shoots me a wink through his lowered window. "Put it on my tab, Ma!"

I try to push away, but the cart wheel twists, making me lunge into the handlebar with my ribs. The guy peels away, kicking up dust that makes me cough, as the woman shouts, "I'm done covering for you! Don't come back here!"

The woman sighs and then seems to notice me, righting the cart again. She wipes at her damp cheeks. "You're not stealing that cart, are you?"

I shake my head. "I'm borrowing it for a friend."

She blinks at me for a moment and then sighs heavily when someone inside the diner yells out, *"Waitress!"*

"Make good choices!" she calls after me as I jog away with the cart.

3

GERTY

Hayes is out of breath, sweat beading across his face, when he shows up exactly forty-three minutes later. I pop out from behind a tree, and he screams.

"Were you there the whole time?" He mops at his forehead.

I nod. "My folks don't like people coming and going. I didn't want you to try to find me."

"Oh," he says, and I know that means he's heard about my family just like I've heard about his.

I check out the grocery cart. "This'll do." I turn into the woods. "Follow me."

A few minutes later, the cart bumping over roots on the footpath, Hayes says, "Covid, was that when your folks got all . . ." He pauses, working through how to describe Alex and Jennifer. "Survivalistic?"

"You know that's not a word, right?" I say, and Hayes

shrugs. "But to answer your question, not really. They weren't surprised by it." I grab the front of the cart and readjust it when it starts to wobble to the left again. "Pandemics strike pretty reliably every hundred years or so. That's why we already had a stockpile of air filtration masks. Besides, we're pretty good at social distancing."

Hayes doesn't say anything when I pause by a hollow tree. From the gap I pull out my ax belt. I strap that on and switch my school shoes for my hiking boots, then tuck my backpack and my school shoes inside the tree for tomorrow. At the clearing in front of my house, I point out a spot for Hayes to park the cart. Then I pick up a big metal bucket of grain. A cluster of chickens strut around us, clucking at one another and us. "Watch Donald," I warn Hayes, and jerk my chin toward the rooster. "He can be a bully."

Hayes shadows me a little closer.

After feeding the chickens, I drop the bucket with a clack onto the stone patio by the back door of my house. "House" isn't quite the word, I guess. I mean, not to most people, maybe. It looks more like an old hunting cabin that would only be used for a weekend. It's log style, but not the cute kind in fairy-tale book pictures. The house tilts to one side, none of the doors shut all the way, and there's a huge section of the roof that's covered by a black tarp with rocks stacked along the edges to hold it in place. Maybe we'd have better repairs if a car could actually fit back here. But Alex and Jennifer park about a mile away in a clearing behind a few trees, and then they hike to the house. In the winter we use the snowmobile.

They don't trust easy access. Alex and Jennifer say that if someone wants to see us, we need to know they're coming.

I know people think I'm strange, but my parents are next level, even in quirky Rabbit. They're hippies, but not the peace-and-love kind. Climate change and political upheaval will mean everyone will need to raise chickens, milk goats, and pump their own water from streams. According to Jennifer and Alex, this could be any day. Life can change overnight. Jennifer says that a lot. Too often, if you ask me.

But everyone has something that makes them happy. For my mom and dad, it's prepping for end-times.

I know not everyone sees things the way they do. The couple of times I went with Jennifer to Hayes's grandma's house, she kept saying "Bless your hearts" when Jennifer traded her homemade pickles for Doc Louise checking on our goats. Doc Louise is not exactly a vet, but her husband, Hayes's grandpa, was one, so she knows a lot about taking care of animals. He's dead now, and there aren't any other licensed vets in the county, so Doc Louise helps out when people are in a bind.

Alex and Jennifer weren't always like this. We used to have a television and live in a neighborhood and even have birthdays and Christmases. Alex says those were our soft days.

Since clearly Hayes knows about my folks, I'm a little surprised to see him working so hard to hide his shock at what my house is like. Here's what it looks like when someone is trying to stay calm: their nostrils flare a little bit, their smile wobbles, their eyes open way too wide.

I plant both feet and pull to yank open the door. Hayes, the lump, just watches with those big eyes, even though I'm a few inches shorter than him. "Jennifer!" I yell to my mom when I finally get the door open. "I'm going into the woods with Hayes."

Jennifer pops her head out from the kitchen area. She nods to Hayes. "Take your knife, just in case!" She looks a lot like me—two blondish-red braids, freckles, skinny enough to disappear if she turns sideways—except older, taller, and with a baby tied to her back with a long swath of fabric. That's my little sister, Lilith.

"Of course!" I snap, annoyed that she reminded me. As though I'd go into the woods without a blade! I pat the small ax strapped to my belt.

Hayes is blinking at me, a sign of fear. "Want a knife?" I ask him, and pull the one we keep under the doorjamb, flip it in the air so the handle faces him. Hayes shakes his head. I shrug and add it to my belt. "Suit yourself."

"Why are you running toward the fire?" I ask as we tramp over fallen logs, following a narrow deer path to the meadow and toward my secret.

"In the dream, you mean?" Hayes responds.

I roll my eyes and don't answer. Of course I mean in the dream. As though Hayes would run toward fire any other time.

"I don't know." When someone lies, their head jerks to the side, like they're looking for the truth. Hayes isn't telling me the truth. I don't think he's telling himself the truth either.

"You don't think *maybe* it has something to do with what you told Mrs. Freid last week? About your mom being a fire-fighter?"

"Mom's not a firefighter," he mutters.

"Yeah." I hold back a long, thin spruce branch so Hayes can duck under it. "But she used to be. And she wants to be, right?"

Hayes shrugs. We're getting close to my secret. I shiver, and it's definitely not from the cold. It's blazing hot, even through the woods. I'm that excited; we're almost to the edge.

"Where are you taking me?" asks Hayes, shooting a glance at the ax. His hands curl and he flicks his wrists.

"You'll see," I tell him, and Hayes keeps following me, even though Alex says never to go anywhere without knowing what you're going to see, who is going to be there, and how to get out of it.

Our property is on the edge of the woods, so my house and the chickens and the goats and everything else we have are surrounded by tall spruce trees. The rest of our acres spill out onto rolling, rocky land like most of Rabbit. It's full of sparse juniper and spiky plants that want to trip you and snakes that want nothing to do with you but will strike if you step on them.

My grandma Nanny Pat lives in a real house with square corners and an actual kitchen filled with food from the grocery store. Here's a bonus secret: Nanny Pat keeps me supplied with my unnatural-food fix: Doritos. Jennifer would freak if she knew, but I believe that orange, powdery cheese is worth the harm of a processed food chain. She and Alex also don't know that Nanny Pat is helping me with my secret, the one that's on a giant tarp in the big pole barn beside Nanny Pat's house.

"C'mon," I tell Hayes as we round the barn.

"Is that . . . ," he gasps, and then stands with his mouth hanging open when he sees it.

"Yep."

I'm building an airplane.

The ultralight looks like a skeleton waiting for tissue to knit it together. Spread out on a huge tarp, the pieces are about where they should be when it finally takes three-dimensional shape. My ultralight isn't one of those preformed kits that anyone could build. Mine is unique. The only pieces I bought are the steel rods (Nanny Pat helped me weld them); the engine, yanked from an old Volkswagen, not installed yet; the epoxy and wood glues; and the windshield. The rest I salvaged.

I squat in the middle of the tarp, staring at the wooden ribs. I need twenty-four exact ribs to build the wing. So far I've got fourteen. I've already tested each of them, hanging them from the two-by-four frame Nanny Pat and I built, and then dangling weights from them. She told me that I needed to prove to her that the epoxy and glue would hold. One hundred fifty-five pounds per rib in, she believed me.

But if Hayes were to build one of the ribs? No way would it hold. In the hour he's been here, Hayes has tried to help me build one. I glare toward the bandage on his thumb. He somehow managed to spear himself with a half-inch-long splinter of plywood. I sprayed it with the antiseptic stuff in Nanny Pat's emergency kit, which was probably over the top for a splinter, but I also kind of wanted to inform him about how quickly infection can set in when an injury is allowed to fester. (Inflammation can start in as few as twelve hours!) Now he's sort of lurking near me, holding the instructions.

I've got to know this airplane inside and out if I'm going to be the one behind the stick. It's not enough to master how to fly; a survivalist must know how to re-create. (That sounds like something my dad would say, but I made it up just now.) The ultralight is taking shape, but there's still a huge spread of pieces, a whole lot left to do.

"Want me to read you the instructions again?" Hayes asks. He's leaning against the barn wall and holding my Doritos, pulling them out one by one. If he licks his fingers before reaching in the bag again, I'm going to throw a wrench in his face.

I've got to calm down. *Focus. Take stock.* "No, I need to know how to do this," I tell him. "I need to commit the instructions to memory so I'm not reliant on a piece of paper."

"But the paper's right here." Hayes holds up the binder with the instructions and waves it in the air, smudging the cover with delicious fake cheese. "The steps are online, too." I don't glance at him. *Online.* As though I'd just *google* ultralight building in the middle of the wilderness. Maybe order a part on *Amazon.* Hayes has a lot to learn.

I close my eyes, concentrating. I wish I had a photographic memory like my dad. I've already read the instructions from front to back three times.

"You know," Hayes says, "an airplane might be something you want to do step by step. It'd be real bad to mess up, I think." He munches on a Dorito, and my grip on the wrench tightens.

Hayes clears his throat. "I had to put together a dresser from IKEA once, for Charlie. I read all the instructions and thought I had it down, but I put the drawers on backward and had to fix it, and then he could never open it without jerking them out so hard that he fell over, which was kind of funny, but it didn't really work well, and maybe this airplane isn't the thing to—"

"Give me the instructions." I put down the wrench and hold out my hand. Friends are overrated. I lunge forward and grab my Doritos too.

I scan the paper again, trying to take a picture with my brain. Nanny Pat will be out soon. She told us she had to finish her "program" on television first. I want to be farther along on this by then. Far enough along that Nanny Pat gives me one of her rare nods and slow blinks.

Hayes grabs the bag of chips as soon as I set it down. "Maybe you should just tell your parents. About the plane, I mean. Maybe your dad could help you with this," he says. "I saw the chicken coop. He built that, didn't he? Maybe this could be something you can do together."

My patience isn't solid to start with, but this is too much. I glare at him. "You don't have a dad or any adult male figures in your life, so you probably don't know how bad what you just said is. But I'm only excusing it once."

Hayes's mouth opens and closes. He rubs the back of his neck, and I feel a little guilty. Maybe it's not entirely Hayes's fault that he thinks of building stuff in a garage as *dad* stuff. Maybe for many kids that's the case.

"My mom built the coop with my help," I snap.

"Sorry," he mutters.

"My dad built our *house*," I add to emphasize my point. There aren't any tarps held down with rocks on the chicken coop, is all I'm saying. Jennifer and Alex have been arguing over the house's construction for years. Jennifer wants to insulate it with hay bales and build with clay; Alex wants nothing that can't be quickly torn down and rebuilt when we need to leave due to imminent disaster, climate change, or government interference. He works at a junkyard and is constantly bringing home stuff that he thinks could go toward fortifying the house. Rarely does any of it actually help. But the pile is great for pilfering from without him noticing. That's how I got most of the wood for the wing.

I shrug and breathe out all the frustration the way Jennifer taught me (fill your lungs with sweet air, picturing the annoying stuff gathering together like a dust bunny; then blow it out and away). "It's okay. Anyway, Alex doesn't have an appreciation for aviation. His focus is wilderness navigation."

Hayes hands me the bag of snacks. His mouth is twitching, and I can see the pulse in his neck is elevated. Probably panicky dust bunnies he's trapped, hopping around under his skin.

"Besides," I say, "this is something between me and Nanny Pat. She's the reason I'm a pilot to begin with." I glance behind me to the back of the pole barn. "See that plane? It's her Cessna. Nanny Pat used it in the 1960s as part of CAP, the Civil Air Patrol. She patrolled on a search and rescue team, seeking out lost hikers as part of the Utah Wing. I'm going to be in CAP like her."

Nanny Pat still wears a little bandana tied in a knot around her neck. She has the same small, slight build as me. But unlike my (and Jennifer's) long red hair and pale face with freckles, Nanny Pat has tanned skin and silver hair. She always wears deep red lipstick, too. I can picture her with goggles and a leather hat covering her ears, sporting her bomber jacket.

Maybe she'll give me a jacket like that once I finish the ultralight.

"CAP?" Hayes asks.

I nod. "Nanny Pat says it's up to me to carry on the tradition. She was a CAP pilot, and so was *her* mother, Lois, who served during World War II. Great-Nanny Lois moved to the East Coast so she could protect boats from missile attacks by German submarines. Did you know that happened? Most kids—most people—don't. History books don't teach the whole story." That's maybe the one thing that Alex, Jennifer, *and* Nanny Pat agree on. I read through the instructions some more while Hayes plays on his phone, finally putting aside my Doritos.

"Wow!" says Hayes, staring at his phone a few minutes later. "German subs *did* attack US boats during World War II. CAP pilots and regular pilots kept the shores safe, like you said."

I stifle annoyance at being fact-checked. Verifying information is another important life skill. I should be proud of Hayes. "And most of them were women," I say instead, feeling my chin point up with the words. That's another part history books tend to skip over.

The flying tradition leapfrogged my mom to me. Jennifer and Alex know Nanny Pat has taken me to flying lessons at the local aviation yard—being able to fly is a powerful survival skill. They do *not* know how much time I spend hanging out in the airport clubhouse, talking to the old pilots about how to build and how to fly. They also don't know about the ultralight.

They especially don't know they helped pay for it, with

money that they had buried in the woods "for the future." (In my defense, they didn't say *whose* future. And they're always telling me that opportunities must be seized. To use everything at my disposal.) They definitely do not know and would not approve of me joining CAP. While you don't need a pilot's license to fly an ultralight, no one can get a license until they're sixteen. But you can be a CAP cadet as soon as you turn twelve. Nanny Pat says if I wait to fly my plane until I have my license, she'll pay for my CAP fees. When we made the deal, she thought it would take me years to build my plane.

I'm going to be twelve in a week and a half. That gives me ten days to think about how I'm going to get Alex or Jennifer to sign the CAP forms.

"I don't get it," Hayes says a few minutes later. He has a habit of randomly starting conversations as though they've been ongoing. I kind of like that about him. Everything he says seems to end with a comma. "If flying is okay, why wouldn't your parents be okay with the CAP thing?"

"Well, think about it," I say, my eyes snatching on a smudge of grease on the tip of my nose. Did you ever notice that if you think about seeing your nose, you can't stop seeing it? "If I join the Civil Air Patrol, then I'm basically joining a government organization. I mean, my squadron would have meetings at the National Guard! To Alex and Jennifer, government equals *bad*. Survival means being independent, standing alone, not part of a squadron."

"I really don't get how your parents think they can take on the entire government," Hayes scoffs. "Were they always like this?"

My mouth fills with spit. It's a natural reaction, the body's way of trying to wash away something that a person shouldn't digest. Sometimes brains get confused and mark thoughts the same way. "No," I say softly.

The screen door to Nanny Pat's house clicks shut, and her shoes hit the hard dirt with a series of clacks as she makes her way toward us.

"They don't think they're going to take on the government." I force a laugh. "They think they're going to avoid it. If they're off the government radar, they'll be free when everything . . ." I push my hands together and then out with wiggling fingers, like an explosion.

Hayes crosses his arms. "They know about tanks, right? That the government has those?"

"Here in Rabbit, we've got Chief Skip and two police officers. I think we'll be all right." Despite everything Alex tells me about police states, Chief Skip seems like a good enough person. He tosses the football to older kids before school, and all the little kids love to give him high fives. He has a wide smile, too, but his eyes are too big, and his forehead wrinkles when he sees Hayes. Sometimes I feel like he sees too much. I don't love that. I like being the one who notices the most.

Nanny Pat strides in with her heels clacking louder now that they are on the cement slab of the barn. I know she isn't wearing a uniform, not really, but she always looks as though she is—today she's wearing dark blue pants, dark leather loafers, a lighter blue button-down shirt, and that little scarf at her neck. "Where are we at, Gerty? Did you secure the tail wheel?"

I assume position, standing with my hands at my sides and my back stiff. "Tail wheel in possession. Currently committing the instructions to memory, Nanny Pat," I say, clipping off my words like a soldier addressing a general.

She glances behind me to where Hayes is standing with the grocery cart. Her eyebrows peak and then she nods. That's a pretty warm greeting from Nanny Pat. She rocks back on her heels and clasps her hands behind her. "Aren't the instructions printed right there? Afraid you're going to forget how to read?" Her stern face softens as she stands in front of the ultralight, nodding a bit. "The speed fairing kit I ordered arrived yesterday, and I installed it last night," she says, holding up a hand when my mouth pops open. She's an engineer and has been inspecting the build, but she shouldn't have been working without me. And she shouldn't have bought a kit without telling me. "I know, I know. It costs more. Consider it an early birthday present."

I fight to keep my face smooth, not to give any tells on how bothered I am. The kit will make the plane soar another ten knots (about eleven and a half miles per hour), plus it will slow how fast my fuel burns. And I don't usually get birthday presents anymore.

But I want the plane to be something that is only *mine*.

Nanny Pat helping? It makes it *ours*. Maybe she'll want to take its first flight, since I'll be waiting for years. The plane seats only one.

For a moment we don't speak. Hayes shifts next to us. Nanny Pat points to the loose hinge. "That's wrong. You need to fix it."

"Yes, Nanny Pat."

She stands there another moment. "It's your mother's birthday today," she says.

"We don't celebrate birthdays anymore," I remind her. Hayes gasps, but we both ignore him. "Alex says it makes people soft. Besides, being born isn't much of an achievement. I was there when Lilith was born. I know who did the work."

Nanny Pat's nostrils flare. "I'd wish her happy birthday if she spoke to me."

"You could fix it. Say you're sorry." The words are out of my mouth before I can think better of them. Nanny Pat's eyes widen. Hayes takes a shuffling step back, like he wants to be part of the wall now. "If you wanted to, I mean," I add.

Nanny Pat crosses her arms. "I don't have anything for which to apologize. Fix that hinge if you're so worried about making things right." Then she marches from the pole barn in short, clacking steps.

4

HAYES

I saw this book one time where every page was blank except for a little drawing in the right corner. If you flipped through it real fast, the stick figure guy moved around like a movie. But it only worked if every picture was just a teeny bit different from the one before. If someone flipped through my mind, it wouldn't make a movie. Every thought ping-pongs around. Every page is wildly different from the one before it.

Worse than that is when one thought won't budge, pasted down like a stamp on the inside of my skull.

That's what happened when Charlie and I first came to live with Grandma Louise.

Mrs. Freid says some thoughts are throwaways. Like say you're just sitting there, minding your own business in math class, and it suddenly occurs to you that the roof might cave in. Maybe not during class or anything.

But sometime it might. And maybe you'll be trapped under it. What then? No one can tell you what happens next because no one else is even thinking about the roof. Even though it's got to be super heavy and it's just hanging there, over your head, all the time.

That's what gets me about some thoughts, including the big one. The one about death. I try not to think about that one the most. I hate when no one knows for sure what happens next.

Mrs. Freid says everyone has dark thoughts, which surprises me. No one else in Rabbit Public School plants their sweaty hands on their desk, presses their forehead between them, and tries to claw at pasted-down ceilings-might-crumble thoughts inside their head, I'll tell you that.

Mrs. Freid says for most people, thoughts pop out of the brain and plop onto an assembly line. Each thought passes by inspectors called the nervous system. If it's a junk thought that isn't going to help a person survive or learn or grow, the inspectors crumple it and toss it in the trash pile, and the brain incinerates it. Only, for some people, such as yours truly, the junk thought sails right by the inspectors. Then it travels through glue, flops off the assembly line belt, and is pasted to the inside of my skull.

Mrs. Freid says I need to crumple the thought and toss it in the trash myself. I try. Sometimes I try so hard that my hands curl with the effort of balling up that thought. No one notices, except for Gerty. And she just watches, doesn't tell me to stop or anything. Gerty is easy to be around. I know she probably only hangs out with me because both of our families are odd and because Mrs. Freid keeps lumping us together. But maybe she could be my friend. Maybe I even had fun hanging out with her today.

I'm walking back from the barn, picking up the pace a little to get back to Grandma Louise's before the porch light turns on. But inside my head I'm peeling off another dark thought. It isn't the thought about how Gerty probably isn't going to want to hang out with me once she has a whole squadron. I think that thought is a reasonable one that inspectors should let by. I need to consider what I'm going to do without Gerty.

Nope, the sticky, sneaky thought I'm trying to scrape away is that someday I'm going to be alone. Completely alone. Without anyone at all. Maybe not today, but someday.

Grandma Louise's rule is that I must be back to the house before dark. Mom doesn't have any rules, not yet. She's probably working on them, though. She's been back only about three months. For about half a year before she left, I was the one who made the rules, even though I was eight. Sometimes I remind Charlie to thank me for not having scurvy like a pirate. I made sure he ate a vegetable every day. And it wasn't easy, I'll tell you that.

I'm not alone.

The sun is setting when I trudge down Grandma's dirt driveway, so I guess I'm cutting it close to curfew. The windows of the small white house are open, and I can hear Charlie talking about a video game and smell the hamburger Grandma is browning for tacos. I stand outside the screen door to kick off my shoes; another one of Grandma's rules is no one wears shoes in the house. I put them right next to Charlie's. Grandma's clogs are beside them.

I'm not alone.

I'm making my mind focus instead on my math homework (and whether I'm going to do it). So I don't notice Mom at first.

She's sitting on the rocking chair, staring out over the sunset. "Hayes," she says, and I nearly jump out of my skin. She smiles and nods toward the empty seat beside her. "Join me?"

I don't want to. But Charlie's laughing in the kitchen and Grandma's going to tell me to wash up. I sigh as I sit down.

"Long day?" says Mom, her voice mocking, as though it'd be impossible for a kid to be tired. I don't answer. "Pretty, isn't it?" She's looking at the sunset, at how the huge sky is streaked with red and orange, the sun a swollen, sinking button in the middle. Her dark hair is pulled in a ponytail at the top of her head, strands springing out.

"I had this dream," I hear myself saying. "Last night, I mean. There was a fire, and I was running toward it." Her jaw clenches but she doesn't look toward me. "But it kept getting farther away. I couldn't reach it."

She stands. "I'm going inside. Time to wash up for dinner."
She probably thinks the dream is about her too.

Saturday morning is blazing. Sweat collects on my forehead,
and I brush my hair back with my fingers so I don't look like
Charlie, whose bangs form a damp upside-down triangle above
his nose.

The farmers market in Rabbit runs on Saturdays from May
through October. Grandma never misses market day. It's
always the same. Someone plucks at a guitar next to a dog
crate with a giant black-and-white rooster inside. His wife
(the guitarist's, not the chicken's) sits on a lawn chair under an
umbrella and sells eggs for three dollars a carton.

"How about plums, Grandma? Plums? We could get plums."
Charlie pulls on the hem of Grandma's T-shirt as they pass
a fruit stand. She's holding a giant straw basket that used to
make me embarrassed based on the size of it alone—Charlie
could probably crawl inside—but that was before I stopped
caring about stupid stuff. The only thing at the market bigger
than Grandma's basket is her matching straw hat.

Remember Nanny Pat in her crisp slacks and button-down?
If she and Grandma stood next to each other, it would be like
those kindergarten worksheets where little kids have to point
out all the opposites. Grandma is tall and broad, her shoulders
wider than any football player's in the NFL. Today she's wear-

ing a loose T-shirt covered with printed flowers, yellow gardening clogs on her feet (with socks), and cutoff denim shorts. Pap was short and narrow, with a face full of angles, and Mom ended up being a mix of them both—as tall and strong as Grandma, but as lean and angular as Pap.

Mom lingers behind me at a stand with late-season peaches. "C'mon, Tara," Grandma scolds her. "Those peaches are past their prime." The stand owner scowls at Grandma's back and sighs when Mom pops one of the sample slices into her mouth.

Mom smiles at the stand owner, and his face softens. When I reach for a sample, Mom whispers, "Grandma's not wrong." I pull my hand back.

I trot a little to catch up with Charlie and Grandma but pause when I see a cluster of three firefighters standing at another table in the market. Though it's wrenchingly hot, they're wearing the bottom half of their gear—fire-retardant yellow pants, boots, and suspenders—and helmets. They're handing out flyers. One holds a megaphone. He bellows, "Donations needed! Almost wildfire season!"

Charlie stops so fast, Grandma bumps into him. "My mom's a firefighter!" He bounces a little, then runs over to them. "Tell them," Charlie says over his shoulder to Mom. "Tell them how you saved all those people!"

Mom brushes against my side as she moves toward them. "Mom . . . ," I mutter, but then follow her instead of Grandma.

Chief Skip, the police officer who throws out pitches for the

Little League, sees Mom and pauses, then slows his steps toward the firefighters. It's only a second, but I recognize the flash of understanding on his face—he knows about Mom. About me.

Mom ruffles Charlie's hair and then puts her hands in her pockets. She rocks back on her heels for a moment before approaching the table. One of the firefighters gives a nod and a half smile. He lifts the can they're using for donations, thinking Mom's about to drop some coin. But her jaw sets, and he lowers the can. Mom's long, dark hair hangs down to her waist. It must be sticking to her back, but she doesn't pull it up. She lifts her chin. "Are you adding firefighters?" she asks, and I hold my breath.

"We're not a volunteer department, ma'am," the second firefighter says. He looks a little older, with a salt-and-pepper beard around his face. Chief Skip crosses his arms, his hip leaning against a market pole. His dark eyes are pinned on Mom's face, and I wish Gerty were here to tell me what his expression means.

"I'm trained," Mom says. Her voice is firm. She pulls back her shoulders. For a moment she reminds me of Gerty. "I fought the Canyon wildfire in California last year."

"Which position?" the younger firefighter asks in the same tone eighth-grade boys use when a girl says she likes a football team and they start quizzing her for stats.

Mom's shoulder blades pop out as she swallows a sigh. "I set the line. Second saw."

The man's mouth twitches, but he doesn't say anything. The older firefighter glances at Chief Skip, who lowers his head when Mom's gaze cuts to him. "You're welcome to apply," the firefighter says. "We could use experienced people."

Mom's chin rises another fraction of an inch. Chief Skip straightens. Mom clears her throat. "I'm trained, and I have recommendations. I'm good. Really good. It's the only thing I've ever been good at." Why is that sentence so sharp?

The firefighter nods, a smile flashing across his face. "I know the feeling." He hands Mom a clipboard with an application attached. "Fill this out. We'll check references, do a background check, and be in touch for the interview."

Mom glances down at me and then to the firefighter. "I have a record. That's where I was trained, as part of job readiness, rehabilitation services. My commander said I was the best prospect she ever trained." Mom straightens a little. "They call it job readiness, but the record—"

"What was the charge?" The firefighter rubs at his beard with his knuckles, eyes drifting down to the clipboard.

Mom pops the cap on the attached pen and begins filling out the form. "Larceny."

"Misdemeanor? That shouldn't be a problem, so long as there isn't anything else." He smiles. "We all make mistakes, right?"

Chief Skip shoots me a grimacing smile, the way someone would do if they saw a little kid's scoop of ice cream topple from a cone. Mom shakes her head. "Felony grand."

Chief Skip rubs the back of his neck as the firefighter winces. "Ah, man. Judges, making examples," he mutters.

Mom shakes her head. "No, sir. I deserved it." She doesn't look up from the clipboard. "But I've served my time."

She fills out the form, even as Chief Skip and the firefighter look at each other and then back to the ground. Even though we all know it's useless.

My thoughts fly off the belt in my brain.

I try to crumple the first one. Felony grand larceny is taking something valuable with no intention of giving it back.

Crumple. Sal Caruso punched me in the gut on the first day of second grade because he wanted my pudding cup.

Crumple. Most of the walls in Sal's house were painted white. The kitchen island was huge, the size of our entire kitchen, and topped with white marble, the gray swirls throughout it like the smoke from a match. Mrs. Caruso smiled whenever I walked through the door and always gave me a hug. When she said, "I'm so happy you're here!" I believed her so much that I went home with Sal after school almost every day.

Mrs. Caruso always had a plate of cut-up fruit and pretzels

in the middle of the island, waiting for us. She hummed along with the radio or talked on the phone on the other side of the island while we did homework. We always did our homework first thing. Then we went to the backyard, where Sal had extra skateboards and scooters.

When he got home, Mr. Caruso would change out of his suit into track pants and throw the football for us. He threw it twice as often to me, but Sal never said anything about it. Sometimes Sal would sigh, and Mr. Caruso would give him a look and I'd know. They had talked about me, maybe about how I didn't have a dad who came home after work to play football. How maybe Charlie and I didn't have cut-up fruit on a tray waiting for us on a big island of marble.

But it never made me feel bad, not like they were judging me or Mom. In fact, when Mom picked me up after swinging by the after-school program for Charlie, she would come into the kitchen too, and I knew it was for one of Mrs. Caruso's hugs. She gave great hugs. "I'm so happy you're here," she'd say to Mom, just like she had to me.

We both believed her.

We believed her so much that when she invited me to go to Disneyland with her, Mom said yes. We believed her so much that when she said I could keep some pj's and a change of clothes in the guest room, I did, because we all knew I'd be spending the night on Friday, and later, when things got bad, Saturday, too.

Crumple. Things got bad because of a backache.

When Mom asked why I never invited Sal to our house, I remember looking around our apartment, its dark brown paneling and the tiny living room. The next day Mom came home with a can of yellow paint. "It'll transform it!" she said. "Make it so bright, we'll feel like we're in the middle of a lemon."

But the paint—named Sunshine Sherbet—dried to the color of old pee. "It's the popcorn ceiling," she said, and pointed to the nubbly texture. "It captures all the light."

She stood on a ladder and sprayed it over and over with fabric softener until our whole apartment smelled like the laundromat on the corner. She scraped it with a little metal tool she had bought at the hardware store, and the pieces fell like the heavy snow I saw in Hallmark movies. "Just wait, Hayes," she said. "We're going to make this place so bright and happy."

Over and over she'd climb and scrape. Move the ladder, climb and scrape. I asked if I could help her, and she said, "No, I've got this!"

Mrs. Caruso invited me over for the weekend. "Bring Charlie, too," she said. "Give your mom some space for her reno project."

Charlie sat at a stool in the kitchen, talking endlessly to Mrs. Caruso, while Sal and I kicked around the soccer ball in the front yard.

When Mom came to get us on Sunday, she rubbed her back

and neck. She didn't squeeze when Charlie hugged her. Mrs. Caruso gave her the name of her doctor.

Crumple. I was reaching for a cup and knocked over the pill bottle. It was by accident, I swear. The little white mounds spilled down the sink. Mom scraped her fingers, trying to reach into the drain. It was the first time I saw her cry.

Mrs. Caruso's doctor wouldn't write another prescription.

But a different doctor did.

Until none of them would.

Crumple. The police checked my locker.

That's how I knew someone had lifted Mrs. Caruso's diamond tennis bracelet, right out of the jewelry box on her gray dresser.

I was in art class. Sal was at my table. We were supposed to be making fall shadow boxes using glue and leaves and sticks. Sal and I kept pelting acorns at each other. Miss Garrison said she'd give us a warning if it happened again, but a few seconds later one smacked me in the top of the head and Sal cackled in the corner.

"Police!" someone said as they walked in holding the giant wooden bathroom pass. "They're searching someone's locker!"

Over Miss Garrison's orders to get back to work, the whole

class rushed to peek from the door. Sal got there before me. His ears flushed red, and his eyes slid to mine over his shoulder. My lunch box, the red one Mrs. Caruso let me borrow once and I never gave back, all my worksheets, my Big Trees sweatshirt, all of it spilled into the hall. The principal glanced up from where he stood behind the two cops, arms crossed. His eyes hardened when he saw me. Then Miss Garrison shut the door and ordered us back to our seats.

Crumple. They searched my backpack.

My pockets, too, but that happened in the principal's office.

Crumple. Mom came to get me, and then they searched her car. It was in the glove box.

Crumple. Later, a long time later, I realized Mrs. Caruso must've given the police my name. She must've thought I was the one who had stolen her bracelet.

Maybe she hugged everyone the same way.

5

GERTY

A weird thing about school is the gaga pit.

When I started going to school last year, I thought the kid showing me around the building was messing with me when she pointed to the huge hexagon in the middle of the dirt-packed recess area. "Oh, that's the gaga pit," she said super casually, like that's a normal sentence.

Those types of *Is this real life?* moments happened a lot those first few weeks. Some things still don't make sense (I'm looking at you, lunch lady serving me "turkey ham" sandwiches). But it turns out that gaga is a game where you stand like a gladiator in that chest-high hexagon and either get hammered by or dodge playground balls other players throw to the ground in a way that they're sure to slam into you.

My reflexes are incredible, though.

I grin a little, thinking about that first day when I stepped into the gaga pit. I skipped, twisted, and leapt out of the way of every ball thrown toward me. Once I grabbed the ball, it took me fifteen seconds to execute four perfect head shots, which, according to the principal, were "not allowed" and "excessively violent" and "not even how the game is played."

Jaxson had a red splotch in the middle of his forehead for an hour.

I'm banned from the gaga pit.

Hayes and I sit under a picnic table beside the playground, not talking to each other.

I don't know if I'd call him a friend, really. I suspect we simply dislike each other less than we dislike everyone else. Okay, maybe the truth is that everyone else dislikes us more than they dislike everyone else. Either way, we've been hanging out together after school now too. And he's been helping me build the plane. (By "helping," I mean handing me tools. Most of the time the wrong ones, but I like that he tries.) I'm nearly finished. I might even finish the ultralight tonight.

I want to tell Hayes that it's almost finished, but I also don't. Once it's done, my plan isn't going to be just an idea. It'll be real. And the next step—telling Alex and Jennifer about it and CAP—is going to be even harder than building a plane. Plus, I don't know if Hayes will still follow me when I turn from the bus toward our woods if the plane is finished. I swallow. Alex says survivors compartmentalize feelings so they can take action. They regulate their breathing—three counts in, five counts out. I practice until I stop thinking about how this year's squadron of CAP members must turn in forms by the end of the week, until I stop remembering that ultralights are responsible for more aviation crashes than any other craft, until I forget how sweaty and flushed Alex was when he buried all that cash that I dug up to pay for my plane.

And it nearly works. Or maybe it's just that I'm distracted by how Hayes's face keeps twisting, his jaw clenching and nostrils flaring. I know he doesn't know how to regulate his feelings the way that I do, thanks to Alex and Jennifer's training. His mind is snagged back to what happened before lunch.

"Do you want to talk about it?" I ask. He knows what I'm referring to and shakes his head. Mrs. Wayne, the math teacher, crossed her arms and stood over his desk. She peered at him while he took his math quiz—a different one from the test the rest of us had finished a few moments earlier. He had gotten 100 percent on that one, and she was sure he was cheating, so she had written new problems on a piece of paper and made him take that one too. "It makes no sense that you would suddenly know how to multiply fractions, when you could barely track the order of operations last week," she had sneered.

I didn't say anything in class, even as Hayes's face flushed and his hands flicked again and again. "I studied," he muttered. But I saw the big ink score Mrs. Wayne wrote at the top of his different quiz: 85 percent. I bet Hayes made sure he messed up some answers, just to get her off his back.

I wanted to say more—like that last month Hayes had slept through every class, but this week he had paid attention. That we had done our homework together, working through the problems while he ate too many of my chips. That if a teacher is going to go on and on about trying your best, then that same teacher shouldn't harass a kid who listens to her. That it isn't right that people expect him to be a cheat because they know his mom has been in jail. But I didn't; the words clogged in my throat. I push some of them loose.

"Mrs. Wayne sucks." I grab a fistful of the long grass growing along the picnic table legs. The blades are thick, more like yucca than lawn. I straighten a few so they're lined up and bend a twist (Alex calls this a "bight") to the side. Then I braid the blades, folding and rolling them, pushing them toward the bight. After a few twists I grab more grass and keep adding to the rope.

Hayes looks away, not reacting to my words, but I know he hears me from the way his jaw tightens. I nudge him.

The sun is streaming down, the breeze pushing around the limbs of the apple tree in the playground, shooting spears of light onto his face. Hayes winces as it flashes over his dark eyes.

His hands curl and open, his wrists flicking. Jennifer says repetitive movements are fine in non–survival situations, that they help alleviate inner turmoil. She says everyone does them. But Alex says *every* situation is a survival situation; you're always a single bad decision away from disaster. They're not exactly optimists, my parents.

Hayes shifts beside me, leaning forward slightly as something captures his attention. I follow Hayes's eyes across the recess field to where his brother is playing. Charlie runs across the field, kicking a soccer ball in quick, steady strides. He's smiling wide, the sun pouring down over him enough to make his hair look like a golden halo. I wonder if Hayes ever smiles like that, happiness pouring through him like sunshine. As though he's never worried about a thing. Beside me, Hayes tenses as Jaxson trots toward Charlie. Jaxson shoots out an elbow and twists his leg to get the ball. Charlie laughs, the side of his foot hitting the ball just enough to pop it away from Jaxson, and keeps dribbling down the field.

Hayes leans back, his legs stretched out and elbows on the table. Here's what it looks like when someone is proud: chin tilts upward, lips stretch back but not apart, eyebrows slightly rise. Hayes's hands rest in soft fists.

Charlie scoops up the ball with the top of his foot, kicking it to his arms. He and four other kids are at the edge of the gaga pit. They are too far away to hear what they're saying, but soon Charlie drops the ball and kicks it lightly out onto the field, and they hop inside the pit.

"What?" Hayes snaps at me.

I startle, eyebrows raised. Here's the thing: I know what he's asking, even if he got the word wrong. He's asking *why*, as in why am I watching everyone so carefully? I shrug rather than answer. The truth is, I'm studying him and his brother. The purpose of going to school, Alex told me, is to see how "regular" people live so I understand his and Jennifer's decision to opt out of society. By the end of this school year, Alex thinks we'll be entirely self-sustaining. "Be an anthropologist," he told me back in June as Jennifer moaned over the school paperwork she had to sign. "Look at the evidence in front of you, use your skills, and reach a conclusion."

I know the scientific method. An experiment is flawed if the researcher is trying to prove a conclusion rather than allowing the experiment to reveal its own evidence. But Alex still thinks that by the end of this school year, I will be done with society at large.

Watching Hayes and his brother, I think he's probably right. Regular people are too complicated.

Pain flits over Hayes's face, and I don't know why. Is it the math class? Is it the way his brother is shining? Something else altogether?

Hayes clears his throat. "I showed Mrs. Wayne I could do the math. Again." Hayes nabs some long grass under the table and hands it to me. I don't point out that what he gives me is too weak for the rope to be decent.

"Yeah, but aren't you mad about it? I'd be pretty angry."

"Oh, are you Mrs. Freid now?" His words are sharp, but the corner of his mouth twitches.

"Anger is a feeling, Hayes," I singsong in a bad imitation of Mrs. Freid. "And every feeling is . . ."

I wait for him to join in with "temporary," but he doesn't. He stands, and then he bolts, barreling toward his brother.

Charlie is pressed against the corner of the gaga pit, Jaxson against him, hissing something in the smaller boy's face. Hayes hurtles over the side of the pit, grabs Jaxson by the shoulder, and tosses him to the ground. I hardly realize I'm on my feet until I'm peering over the edge of the pit, seeing Jaxson scurry backward as Hayes turns to Charlie. Hayes's face is twisted. Here's what it looks like when someone is furious: forehead wrinkles like wings above each narrowed eye, mouth opens in a silent snarl, bottom jaw juts forward.

The gym teacher is on duty, and he comes running, blowing his whistle as Jaxson scuttles like a crab to the other side of the pit. "What is wrong with you?" Jaxson screams.

Hayes flips back to him, arms bent by his sides like a wrestler. "Leave my brother alone," he growls.

"I can take care of myself," Charlie says, but neither Hayes nor Jaxson seems to hear him.

"We're just playing the stupid game," Jaxson says as he scrambles to his feet.

Stay down, stay back, I silently plead with him. The look on Hayes's face—it's a warning, as clear as a bright red berry's promise of poison. But Jaxson stomps toward Hayes. No one seems to hear the teacher's whistle screeching over and over.

Adrenaline rush—I know all about it. Survivors must focus on every detail around them, or their mind edits reality into a story, cutting out the background noises. Jennifer says it's like how moviegoers don't hear loud popcorn chewers when watching the film, but I don't really get that, since I've never seen a movie and loud chewing makes me want to go gaga gladiator on people in the cafeteria.

Jaxson barrels into Hayes, his shoulder ramming into Hayes's chest. Charlie is now pinned between Hayes and the low wall. His face, already flushed with embarrassment, is now slick with tears from pain, too. Neither Hayes nor Jaxson notices. Hayes's fisted hand slams into Jaxson's ribs. This is *bad* bad. The teacher pushes through the crowd of kids watching the fight, all of them buzzing.

"Stop!" I shout, and for some reason it works. Hayes's fist drops to his side. When Jaxson steps forward, Hayes's hands come up to shove him back—but once Jaxson is at a safer distance, Hayes ignores him and suddenly seems to remember his brother. I see the realization flash across his face, the intake of breath and the name on his mouth. He turns to Charlie, seeing his red face, noting how he holds his stomach, understanding he felt the impact of each punch and shove. "Charlie," he breathes, just as the whistle blows so loudly that it could be a siren. Just as Jaxson smashes into Hayes from behind so hard that his head slams forward, whacking Charlie right over his eye. Hayes whips toward Jaxson, but no anger twists his face.

Guilt, I think, and snapshot the expression in my mind. *That's what guilt, maybe even horror, looks like.*

The teacher jumps over the edge of the gaga pit and grabs Jaxson and Hayes in each fist, holding them as though he ripped a single sheet of paper in two.

Mrs. Freid comes barreling out of the school, the lanyard around her neck slapping against her stomach as she runs. The gym teacher's grip on the boys tightens enough that the knuckles of his fists are white against his tan skin. "I've got 'em," he grumbles, his jaw twisting. But Hayes struggles, the neck of his T-shirt stretching as he tries to pull away.

"Charlie!" he says, and though his mouth opens wide as if to yell, his voice comes out as a whimper.

Sprawled in the gaga pit dirt, Charlie holds both hands over his left eye, his legs up as he rocks back and forth on his back. He sobs. *"Mama."*

The word shifts something in Hayes, and he goes still. For a moment I picture him as a tree, roots spilling through his shoes, deep into the dirt, limbs hardened to bark. He seems not to feel the gym teacher's yank of his T-shirt, not to hear anything else anyone says. Until Jaxson laughs, bitter and mean. "Aww, li'l baby wants his *ma—*"

Hayes lunges at Jaxson, ripping his T-shirt as he tackles the other boy. I watch them both rolling in the dirt.

6

HAYES

Feelings are temporary," Mrs. Freid says, her voice soft despite the hard lines of her face. "The anger you felt then, the . . ." She seems to taste different words in her mouth before speaking. Her dark brown eyes narrow as they dart across my face. "The remorse you feel now," she decides, "also is temporary. It's what you do *while* you're feeling them that matters, Hayes."

I nod, figuring it's the best way to get her to stop talking. The ice pack I'm holding against my forehead chills my whole body. I'm so tired. I want to leave. Not just Mrs. Freid's office. Not to go to Grandma Louise's. I want to be alone, be dropped in the middle of nowhere. Somewhere without Mrs. Freid's panicky face, Gerty's watchful eyes, Mom's scowl, or, worst of all, the black smudge over Charlie's eye. I don't want to see anyone.

I don't want to feel anything. I don't want to think about the anger crackling inside me all the time.

She lays her hands on the desk, palms up, as she takes a deep breath. "What do you think would be a *good* way to handle anger?"

In California a couple of sixth graders got into a fight, and it wasn't nearly as bad as what Jaxson and I did. Both of them were expelled. But in Rabbit? I'm not sure what's going to happen. After the nurse told Jaxson he was fine and gave me and Charlie ice packs, Mrs. Freid pulled me into her office. She scowled when Gerty slid through the door behind me but didn't tell her to leave.

I stare at the counselor. She stares at me.

Gerty lounges in her chair beside me, gnawing on a piece of jerky. "This better be good, because I'm pretty sure my dad and mom are going to be handling some anger soon. My birthday is in two days. We don't give presents anymore, and that's okay because all I want is permission for CAP. The sign-ups are due by the end of the week. And tonight I'll probably finish my—"

Mrs. Freid interrupts. "I'm talking with Hayes right now, Gerty. We'll talk about your new hat in a moment." She doesn't move her eyes from me. Gerty nearly told her giant secret. Later I'll wonder why she did it—if it was to give me cover, or if she really was ready to talk about the airplane.

"Uh," I say, "handling anger, you mean, like, *not* shoving Jaxson into the dirt?"

Gerty snorts and Mrs. Freid sighs. "Yes, Hayes. Aside from pushing your friend into the dirt, what would've been a smarter way of handling this situation?"

"He isn't my friend." Mrs. Freid's eyes narrow further, so I continue. "And he was shoving my little brother around. Right, Gerty?"

Gerty sucks on a tooth, probably trying to dislodge the jerky. She shrugs. "I guess so. I didn't see it." Mrs. Freid's head tilts at that. I know why. Gerty sees everything. *Was* Jaxson shoving Charlie around? My mind rewinds to the moment I saw Jaxson hovering over my brother in the gaga pit. Okay, so maybe he wasn't actively shoving Charlie, but it looked like he was going to anytime. "I'm down to the last step," Gerty says. "Nanny Pat says she'll help me talk to Alex and Jennifer, but I actually think that would make it even wor—"

"As it happens," Mrs. Freid says, "Jaxson's parents don't want to press charges for your assault."

"Assault?" Gerty huffs next to me, but I can't turn to see her. I can't move at all. *Charges.* A gavel smacking down, a door clanging shut. They don't send kids to jail for fighting on the playground, right?

Gerty sits upright. She's not looking at me, but I know she's watching all the same. Slowly her hands curl, wrists flick, then open. She repeats the motion, this time even slower. It's what I do when I'm peeling away throwaway thoughts. Gerty turns toward me, just a little bit. I swallow the sourness that flooded my mouth with that too-loud word and then copy her movements.

Mrs. Freid folds her hands on her desk and stares down at them. "I can help you, Hayes," she says softly. "Strong emotions are overwhelming, but if we don't give them fuel, they burn out. There are ways to sit with these feelings, to let them sizzle out."

"Fizzle," Gerty says.

Mrs. Freid ignores her correction. "Meditation, for example." She holds up a slim hand. "Now stop it, don't roll your eyes at me. It works."

Gerty shrugs, turning fully toward me. "She's right. Meditation has been around forever. Samurai warriors meditate on death so they can fight without fearing it."

"I'm supposed to sit here and think about how angry I am, and that will make me not angry?" I groan. "I'm not even angry anymore, okay?"

Mrs. Freid presses her lips together, then says, "Perhaps we could just close our eyes and think of something peaceful. Like a tree. I have a favorite tree that I think about when I want to feel more tranquil."

Gerty, for some reason, straightens. Her focus intensifies in a way that reminds me of a wolf closing in on elk or something. "Tell me about it," she says. "Your tree, I mean."

Mrs. Freid's eyes flare in surprise. Gerty doesn't show a

whole lot of interest in these conversations, generally speaking. "Well," Mrs. Freid says slowly. She reaches behind her and grabs a framed picture from the bookshelf under the window. It's her, but younger, maybe just a few years older than us. She's with her mom. Whoever took the picture must've stood on a bench or something, because the angle is top down. Over her shoulders is a large tree with slender limbs and bright red leaves. The trunk can't be seen; it's growing *below* her, the building behind her designed with a giant open square for the tree to grow in.

"This was taken at my college in Cambridge, Massachu-setts," she says. "There's a library that goes into the ground, and right in the middle is this Japanese maple. The whole building encircles it. When you walk by, the canopy is barely to the top of the enclosure. When you're inside the building, you're technically underground, but all the windows look out into this courtyard where the tree stands, making you feel like you're aboveground."

She swallows, staring at the picture for a beat longer. When she looks up, her expression is already more peaceful. "Any-way," she says, "when I'm feeling overwhelmed, I close my eyes and I think of this tree. Of how, when I was a student with hundreds of pages of reading to do, I could look out and see this tree and feel connected to nature." She twists to put the photograph behind her again. Beside me, Gerty scowls, cross-ing her arms, nostrils flaring.

"That's not a happy tree," Gerty snarls. "Putting it inside a building like that? It's mean."

"What are you talking about?" Mrs. Freid laughs. "It's surrounded by students. Everyone loves that tree."

"Not enough. Trees like being in a forest. My favorite is Pando. He has a root system of more than forty thousand trees. *They're* happy. They're connected. That one is sad."

"Trees can't be sad." Mrs. Freid's voice is sharp.

"You're wrong." She doesn't say it angry, either. Like it's simply a statement. "I'm joining CAP because of Pando. I know a lot about trees."

"Trees don't have feelings, Gerty," Mrs. Freid huffs.

"Trees are—"

"Enough, Gerty!" Her voice is a slap. Mrs. Freid slowly closes her eyes and opens them again. She doesn't look up from her desktop.

Anger flares inside me at how Mrs. Freid snapped at Gerty. "Why shouldn't trees have to feel it too?" My words are almost a snarl.

Mrs. Freid blinks, still not looking up. "Feel what?" Her voice is hollow.

I don't answer her.

"Sad? Angry?" she responds for me. None of us speaks. Gerty's head swivels between us, but her mouth is clenched shut. Eventually Mrs. Freid clears her throat. "How about you, Hayes?" she says as though the previous interaction never happened. "Do you have a favorite tree? One that you've admired or noticed?"

An image slams into me. Crumbling red bark, fissures of black charcoal, towering yet stunted. "No."

The bell rings, and Mrs. Freid doesn't stop us as we leave.

7

HAYES

I can't stop thinking about Mrs. Freid's question. About the tree.

I can't stop thinking about the Mother of the Forest.

Technically, I wasn't lying when I answered Mrs. Freid. She asked if I had a tree I admired. I don't admire the Mother. It actually . . .

I want to say it terrifies me. But that isn't quite right.

The first time I saw it, my stomach cramped for a moment like when I had food poisoning. And that was before I even read the sign in front of it, telling me its story.

Before . . . everything that happened with her . . . Mom took me and Charlie to Big Trees State Park. No one else in the towns nearby went there unless they had a summer job at the park. But Mom said that while we couldn't afford going to Disneyland, we could be tourists in our own town. We did the whole gig. We drove the few miles up the road to Patio Diner. Somewhere buried in her phone is a picture of me and Charlie under a big fluorescent ice-cream cone sign. My arm's around Charlie, his two front teeth missing and his belly pushing against his shorts. Both of us have chocolate ice-cream mustaches. We're smiling so wide.

Mom picked up some granola bars and dried mango from Treats. Then we drove out of the cheesy Old West town past orchard stands. We—all three of us—mooed out the window at the cows clustered in the shade of small clumps of trees. When the road wended along forested hills, we cricked our necks to see the tops of trees.

"They just go up and up and upper," Charlie whispered when we got out of the car by the sequoia grove. He tripped over a root poking through the paved walkway. For a mile and a half, Charlie gushed about these trees, and I tried to play it cool. I don't know why I did that—acted like it wasn't that big of a deal.

But those trees.

The sequoias are taller than buildings. So wide that entire families could circle them. There was a stage in the middle of the grove, but really it was a stump. A hundred or more years ago, someone chopped down that tree. Now people stand on it to get their picture taken. Another forgotten image from years back on Mom's phone, blurry and out of focus, is of her and Charlie. The little twerp is still looking up, mouth open, while Mom stares steadily into the camera.

C'mon, those eyes are saying. *Look, Hayes. Look!*

Mrs. Caruso would've spread sunscreen on our arms and snapped pictures, but she wouldn't have pressed her hands against the soft red bark and closed her eyes as though she were in a temple. (Okay, so I touched the bark too.) Mrs. Caruso wouldn't have pushed her back against the trunk, tilted her head up, and stared at the canopy. *Look, Hayes. Look!*

That's all Mom said to me as we walked. "You know I can see, right?" I snapped at one point. "Mrs. Caruso doesn't get on Sal's case to look at stupid trees." I hated the way she wanted me to see things the same way she did. Other moms we passed took pictures and yelled at their kids not to trip on roots or swat at bees. "Why can't you be normal, like Mrs. Caruso?" I said, and something dark twisted inside me at how the words made her flinch. Mom stopped talking to me after that.

Then we turned the corner, and there was the Mother of the Forest in front of us.

Mrs. Caruso wouldn't have stood in front of the scarred giant with tears burning her face. She wouldn't have shook and sobbed and ruined the day. I wouldn't have had to feel those tears scald my own face.

The Mother is a skinned tree.

One hundred seventy years ago, no one believed that trees could be bigger than dinosaurs and live thousands of years.

Then a hunter chased a grizzly bear into a dense part of the woods where white explorers had never ventured. He wounded the bear but stopped searching for it before finishing it off. That's because he saw those trees and was too shocked to continue.

He told everyone after he got back to camp. No one believed him. He had to trick them to follow him back into the woods. Once they did, they marveled at the trees too. A man who wanted money and fame more than anything else heard them talk about the monster trees.

Soon that man stood amid the sequoia grove in front of the most glorious one of all. The tree that was so strong, they called it the Mother of the Forest.

He didn't cut her down. That would've taken too much effort, and moving her all the way east, where the so-called important people would pay to see her, would cost too much money. So he hired other men to saw swatches of her bark, about a foot thick and taller than a man, from her body. They started where her roots had plunged into the dirt and continued up to her first branch, more than a hundred feet into the air. Each piece of her was numbered and marked, so three thousand miles away they could put the puzzle together for fancy people to marvel at her skin. A massive, scaffolded farce of a giant tree.

But what happened to her?

Her sap slowly bled into the dirt. Without her bark, she

couldn't survive. It took more than a year for her to die.

A fire swept through the area. The other sequoias were strong enough to handle the flames. But she was laid bare, and most of her crumbled. The pieces of her core left behind are black with fire scars.

She was 2,500 years old when she died.

But people continue to walk by the part of her that still stands, locked in place by those roots. "The Mother," they whisper, snapping pictures of her corpse. A blackened, gnarled, ugly reminder of how when someone wants something desperately enough, they'll destroy anything beautiful in their path to get it.

Riding the bus home from school, I shake my head at the memory of the Mother of the Forest. I swear, I can hear pills spilling into the sink, toppling down the drain, see Mom's fingers grasping for them.

I didn't lie to Mrs. Freid. I don't admire this tree. I hate it. I hate how it wears its pain for everyone to see. Hate how no one can pretend they don't see it, how they shake their heads and look at it with pity or maybe even fear when they come across it in the forest. People gaze up at the Mother of the Forest the way Grandma Louise looked at me and Charlie when she picked us up from the group home. The way the firefighters looked at Mom at the farmers market.

Everyone who sees the Mother of the Forest knows it is never going to get better. It's never going to hide its scars.

It's never going to be beautiful again. Everything that made it strong is gone. Forever.

Look, Hayes. Look!

When I stood in front of the Mother of the Forest, I couldn't look at it, not more than a glance. But that glimpse is a postcard stuck inside my mind, one I can't ever seem to claw off the walls of my skull.

"Trees don't have feelings." That's what Mrs. Freid said. I wish I didn't either. It would be so much easier if I didn't.

If I had never told Mom she should be more like Mrs. Caruso, she wouldn't have tried to make our apartment look like a room in Sal's house. If I hadn't spilled that bottle, she wouldn't . . .

I yank at the sticky thoughts, crumple them and force different ones down the conveyer belt in my skull.

I wonder if the man was happy once he was famous.

I wonder if, when he closed his eyes, he saw fancy people and soft bark.

I wonder if he ever went back to look at what he had left behind.

I wonder what happened to the bear, the one that cost the Mother everything when all it did was run.

"We need to talk about the fight, Hayes," Mom says the next day, tucking her cell phone into her back pocket. The principal called to tell her about the fight the day before. Grandma Louise sent me to my room before Mom could say a word. I knew I should've gone with Gerty instead of following Charlie back to Grandma Louise's once the bus dropped us off. "What were you thinking?"

I don't look up from my Chromebook, even though the math problems swirl together and I can't make out the numbers in front of me. "A kid was messing with Charlie."

"Charlie won't tell me anything. Is he getting bullied?"

I don't answer. Charlie didn't talk to anyone on the bus ride home. Didn't say a word to me.

Mom squeezes my shoulder. "Your brother can take care of himself."

I shake her hand off. "You don't know that." *You don't know anything.*

I feel her there, standing too close. "It's not your job to take care of him. I . . . I'm here now, and, Hayes . . . ," she whispers. But anything else she's going to say is cut off with a knock at the door.

Grandma Louise's heavy steps slap against the linoleum floor as she heads toward the door. She has two baby opossums, each the size of an apple, on one shoulder. Someone dropped off a box of them the night before, and only these two are still kicking.

She opens the screen door. "Skip!" Her voice is happy and light. "What brings you here today? I hope not another animal issue in town. The last thing I need is another litter."

Chief Skip. I stand as Mom turns around. He's here for me, I know it. Because I shoved Jaxson. Now I'm going to go to jail. I'm going to be far from Charlie and Mom and Grandma Louise, and nothing is ever going to be the same again. Blood pulses in my ears. My breath is coming so fast, a part of me sees my chest rising and falling, rising and falling. I wrecked everything! *Everything!* I—

And then I notice Mom, shaking in front of me, her fingers stretched and wide in front of her like she's warding Chief Skip away. She steps backward, almost into me. It pins my legs against the table. I lean into her, and she stops trembling. "Why are you here, Officer?" she asks. I swallow some of the sourness in my stomach. Mom's voice is steady. I wonder when she learned how to do that, to keep her voice strong even when her body betrays her fear.

Chief Skip's mouth twitches, and he seems to rub away the inclination to smile with the back of his hand. "Evening, Louise." He nods to Mom. "Tara." His eyes dip to mine, and the soft wrinkles around his eyes deepen. *Does he like this? Arresting people?*

I step to the side. Mom's arm swings low and out, the way she does when she's driving and has to stop suddenly.

"Here as a courtesy." Skip takes his hat off and holds it in his hand, swinging it in slow circles as he talks. He glances toward Grandma, but his eyes dart back to Mom's and lock. "There was an incident nearby. Last night a home on the outskirts of Rabbit got ransacked. Sloppy job; some jewelry stolen. Some electronics."

Mom's chin lifts. She crosses her arms, the muscles tightening. "So naturally you thought to come here." She doesn't sound scared anymore. She sounds tired.

Skip nods, then quickly shifts into a shake of his head. "As a—"

"Courtesy," Mom finishes. "I get it. Suspicion first goes to the felon who recently moved to town. Forget that she served her time and is clean. Forget that she got a transfer of probation and hasn't had a single issue—"

"You got me wrong," Skip interrupts. His voice is clipped now. No wrinkles around his eyes.

"Then why *are* you here?" I ask. I'm being rude. I know I am. But Mom doesn't check me. Her mouth tightens, but she doesn't move. Grandma Louise and the two baby opossums gape at me.

Skip straightens. He swallows and widens his stance. "I came here *as a courtesy* to warn y'all to lock your doors at night. Make sure your vehicles are secure. These jobs tend to cycle through towns. Wouldn't be surprised if another house out here on the edge of town was the next target."

Silence as thick as cotton stuffs the room.

Finally Mom drops her arm. She sucks in her lips and clenches her jaw. Then she nods. "I see. I appreciate your concern."

"Course we all do," Grandma pipes in. "That was mighty kind of you to think of us. I'll make sure we keep an eye out."

"This crew, whoever did this, they didn't seem to have a plan," Chief Skip says. "Broke in, smashed stuff out, took anything remotely valuable. I don't get the sense that they're malicious, but things tend to escalate quickly when folks are desperate. If you see anything, don't engage. Call us."

No one speaks for a moment.

"How about a cup of lemonade?" Grandma says.

Chief Skip again locks eyes with Mom. After a long moment he looks away, shooting a half smile to my grandma. "Another time, Louise."

He turns and Mom steps forward. "Thank you," she whispers.

Chief Skip stalls as though he stepped onto a land mine. He looks over his shoulder at Mom. He nods, then walks off the porch and back to his cruiser.

Mom pauses a breath and then strides toward the door. She never used to move like that. I remember being smaller than Charlie and losing her in a crowd at the mall. I spotted her because she used to bounce with each step. She doesn't do that anymore. Now she strides, steps precise and focused.

Gerty moves like that. I never noticed before this moment. I'm not sure why I do now, as Mom reaches the door.

"Chief," Mom calls. I step forward, catching the screen door before it closes, and step out onto the porch. Mom glances at me, but the smile she gives me is tight.

"Skip," he responds. "That's what everyone calls me. My name is Charles, but no one calls me that. I don't really like the nickname. I wish they'd stop. My brother and I both got saddled with terrible ones. Mom's not too imaginative, I guess. Skip and Sp—"

"I finished probation before I came out here," Mom interrupts. "I made good time inside."

"That's not why I'm here." His voice is gentle. I lean forward to catch his words, they're so soft.

"But I wanted you to know," Mom says. "And . . ." She glances at me again and then steps backward, so she's beside me. Her hand on my shoulder feels like an apology as she says, "A friend, from inside, she finished her probation. Jacey was one of my bunkies . . . cellmates. She's visiting tonight, staying for a few days."

I gasp. "Tonight? Why didn't you tell us?"

Mom swallows. "I didn't want to say anything until Jacey's plans were firmed up. I think . . . I think it'd be nice for you to meet a friend from inside."

"Inside" meant prison. What was Jacey in for? Larceny, like Mom? Or worse? "Why would she come *here*?" I blurt at the same time that Chief Skip says, "You don't have to inform me of your guests."

Mom answers me instead of him. "She's a fire girl too. On my crew, and I miss . . ." Mom's voice trails off, but it's too late. I know what she was going to say. She misses her. She misses *prison*. How messed up is that? A strangled sort of noise squeaks out of me. I shrug off Mom's grasp on my shoulder and stomp back to the house, letting the thin door slam shut behind me. But the screen doesn't block Chief Skip's words.

"I hope you have a nice visit," he says. "Make sure your doors are locked at night."

Mom is back in the house a moment later, trailing me into the kitchen. "Hayes, we need to talk about this." Her jaw tightens. "I was going to tell you at dinner. She and I have been messaging each other. She got permission to leave the state and wants to come here. She helped me a lot—I think it might help you understand . . . me . . . if you met her. If you knew some of our stories—"

"What did she do?" I ask, not looking up from where I'm filling a glass of water at the sink.

Mom swallows. "That doesn't matter. She did her time. Just like me."

"I can't believe you'd bring one of *them* around Charlie." My words are flames. I turn to see if they burn her. Mom's eyes turn to ash.

"That isn't fair, Hayes. You're talking about my friends. About *me*."

"Maybe, for once, you could think about *me*. About what it's like having a felon for a mom. Now you want to bring your so-called *bunkie* around?" I dump the water into the sink without taking a sip and slam the glass on the countertop.

Then I push past her to go to the room I share with Charlie, but he's standing in the hallway.

Charlie's eye is so bruised that it's nearly black. He folds his arms across his chest. "Mom isn't a felon." The way he says the word, I know he's never used it before, that it's unfurling in his mouth, his tongue hating the taste of it. He's looking at me like *I'm* the criminal. "Mom's a firefighter."

I twist and barrel out of the front door.

8

GERTY

I hear Hayes walking up Nanny Pat's driveway and quickly stuff the Doritos bag under the tarp. Then I sit cross-legged in the middle of the ultralight pieces and pretend to read the instructions. I nod to myself to complete the effect. Nanny Pat and I installed the engine the night before. Only a few more steps. I know I don't celebrate my birthday, but it's kind of cool that it'll be done on time for it.

"Why'd you lie to Mrs. Freid?" I say as he walks in. He must've come the long way to Nanny Pat's. Instead of cutting through my woods, he walked a mile and a half through town to the front of my grandmother's house. I'm glad he remembered what I told him about Alex's roving booby traps. I'm glad, too, that he's here, but I try not to dwell on that. Alex says a person can count only on themselves. To depend on others is to be weak.

Hayes pauses in the doorway. He pushes his hand through his hair and then shrugs. I try not to let my eyes snag on the way his cheeks are wet. Is he still upset about the fight at school? He had to spend the day in the principal's office, in-school suspension. Did something else happen?

"You really like to ease into conversations, don't you?" he says.

I raise an eyebrow at him.

He plunks down dangerously close to the hidden chips. "I didn't lie. I thought of a tree—the Mother of the Forest—but I don't *like* thinking about it. It's—"

"An example of how man destroys anything beautiful just because he can?" I interrupt. He gapes at me, and I roll my eyes. "Of course I heard about that sequoia. Alex says it's a symbol of capitalism and that anyone who sees it and still decides to be part of the system is morally corrupt. Jennifer says it's a representation of the patriarchy." I stand and walk over to the plane. The frame is coming together nicely. Next step is attaching the windshield. "Give me a hand?" I ask Hayes. I still when I hear the telltale crinkle of the chip bag as he stands, but he isn't as observant as me and rarely uses all his senses, so he doesn't look under the tarp.

"Did you ever see it in person?" His voice is quiet. "It's . . ." He shakes his head.

I don't like the boiling inside me. I know a lot. *A lot.* Way more than most people my age, and I suspect much more than people my parents' age and older. But I don't know how *not* to be jealous. I can tell Hayes everything there is to know about the Mother of the Forest. But he has *seen* it. He saw it, and the memory of it puts a shadow over his face. It steals his words.

That's a kind of knowing I don't have a lot of, having spent half my life in Rabbit. Alex and Jennifer are suspicious of mass transportation. And since Lilith was born, Jennifer doesn't like to leave home much. So I pretty much only remember seeing Rabbit. Just Rabbit.

But once this plane gets the all clear from Nanny Pat? Then, a couple years later, once I get my license and join CAP, I'll be able to go wherever I want . . . within a radius of about 180 miles. I run my hand along the windshield I'm about to install. It's clear, brand new. Not a single nick.

I don't even need my license to fly the ultralight. There aren't restrictions like that on pilots for these planes. But I promised Nanny Pat I would; it was a condition of being allowed to use her pole barn for construction.

Jennifer says that Nanny Pat likes "conditions." Alex, though I don't know why, calls them "catch-22s." Like when Jennifer was a kid, Nanny Pat's condition for her was that she could wear whatever outfit she wanted, but only if she paid for it herself—yet she wouldn't be allowed to get a job until she graduated. Like Jennifer could marry whomever she wanted to marry, but Alex would never be welcome in Nanny Pat's house.

Conditions are a big reason why Nanny Pat and Jennifer don't talk anymore. Once Alex announced his plans for us to go fully off the grid, he and Nanny Pat had a huge fight. Alex yelled that he was going to make sure his family knew how to live free, independent from the government, without "conditions." Nanny Pat snapped that no one can live on their own, and he was depriving us all of a chance to be part of a community.

Now Alex says Nanny Pat is too entrenched in society to be trusted. Jennifer cried for three days and then decided to listen to Alex instead of Nanny Pat. My mom, she doesn't listen to herself at all. I don't think she even has an opinion about most things. Alex says some people are alphas. If he's an alpha, so is Nanny Pat.

I know the first place I'm going to go when I get my license. I'm going to get away from all of them, my parents and Nanny Pat, and go see Pando.

I grit my teeth, trying to clear my head, and motion to Hayes to help hold the windshield steady while I use Nanny Pat's cordless drill to drive in the screws. While my plane has a windshield, it doesn't have doors. The plane has to be light—no more than 255 pounds—so no doors. The seat is repurposed canvas strips from one of Nanny Pat's lawn chairs, but the seat belt is something else I had to buy. I still have some dirt under my nails from digging up another cache of Alex's money a couple of days ago.

I'm about to ask Hayes about the fight when he says, "Do you have a tree?" He says the words so quickly, they mush together. Shame looks like averted eyes, curled shoulders, bowed head. He's worried I'll make fun of him. And I could. A part of me even wants to, so the boiling jealousy inside me can spill out of my mouth to scald someone else.

And then I choke on a laugh. Here I am *jealous* of Hayes, the only kid who is lonelier than me, whose teachers look *more* concerned when they talk about his "home life," the only one picked *after* me in gym class. But Hayes doesn't know what I'm thinking; he only hears the laugh.

"Forget it," he says, and steps away, the fixed-once-already hinge on the windshield snapping at that spot.

"Stop!" I bark.

I'm a little surprised that Hayes listens. He hoists the windshield back into place and looks at me, waiting.

Caring about what other people think, how they feel, is a luxury survivors don't indulge. That's what Alex says. Survivors care only for their pack, and no way would Alex nor Jennifer think of Hayes as part of our pack, even if he is my friend. *Is* he my friend?

I grasp the edge of the windshield under his grip, our hands brushing. "I was laughing at me, not you." He doesn't say anything while I drill in the next screw. The gap from the broken hinge isn't significant. "Both you and Mrs. Freid actually *saw* your trees, and they're hundreds of miles away from where we are now. Mine is one county over and I've never actually seen it."

I line up another screw and then clear my throat. "The truth is, I don't have a tree. I have Pando."

Hayes doesn't move, barely breathes. That's how I know he's listening. He's like a deer that way. When a thought has his focus, nothing else does. He'd be terrible in an emergency. Alex says survival depends on being able to anticipate any event, to plan for it. Hayes isn't a planner. He's in the moment. I glance at him, nodding that I'm ready to let go of the windshield.

"Who is Pando?" he asks.

"You don't know about him?" Once again I know more than anyone else. "I talked about him with Mrs. Freid. Weren't you listening?"

Hayes sighs and rolls his eyes. I clamp down on a smile.

"Pando is the oldest, heaviest, largest living organism in the world," I say. "And he's right here in Utah."

Some experts say Pando is eighty thousand years old. Others say older than one hundred thousand.

He weighs thirteen million pounds—for real!—and stretches across more than one hundred acres. And he started with one small root. I close my eyes and imagine that I can see him.

But, to tell the truth, no one truly can see Pando. Not what really makes him special. That's all underground.

"Pando is an aspen clone," I tell Hayes. I can tell he doesn't get it, not yet. "Most people who see him think they're in a forest, but they're not. Every tree—all forty thousand of them—is like a strand of hair sprouting off one head. That head, or root system, is Pando."

Highway 25 cuts right through it. People drive by and have

no idea what they're seeing, that they're passing through an ancient giant. "Know what's really wild about him?"

Hayes blinks at me. "That you talk about a bunch of trees like it's a person?"

"No," I snap. "That one of the reasons Pando has lived so long is fire. That region used to get a lot of forest fires. Sure, the flames would kill some of Pando's trunks, but they'd also get rid of anything that competed with him for resources. So he'd just send up more shoots. His roots are strong enough for that."

Hayes swallows. "There are wildfires here?"

I nod. "Every year. Fishlake foresters usually do controlled burns to stay on top of it. There's one a couple hours south of us right now. Nanny Pat heard about it on the radio." I step back, looking at my plane. It's nearly finished.

Sweating is a normal bodily reaction when you're standing perfectly still but thinking about something scary. Such as telling your parents that you want to join a government operation. Or that you maybe might've dug up their hidden stash of money and used it to build an airplane.

"Something's wrong," I say. Hayes's eyes widen, looking at the plane, and I shake my head. "With Pando, I mean. He's dying. Maybe it's climate change. Maybe it's bugs or fungus." I run my gaze along the exterior of my plane. It looks a bit like an insect: a bubble of a body stretching to a point, and a long white wing across the top. "Maybe it's too many ranchers

letting their cattle eat the new shoots. But Pando isn't growing the way he should. Old trees die, and not enough replace
them." I swallow. "I'm going to protect him, though. When
I'm in CAP, I'm going to take care of people and all that, I
guess. But really? I want to patrol Pando. I'm going to go there
and I'm going to know . . ."

"Know what?" Hayes asks.

Fight or flight is a being's response to a body freaking out.
When someone is confronted with something powerful or
scary, they either fight or flee to stay safe. Right now, looking
at my plane, realizing it is finished and that my birthday is
tomorrow? Knowing that means I have to tell Alex and Jennifer about joining CAP and the whole helping-myself-to-their-
buried-money thing? I want to do both. I want to fight to be
heard but I also want to run.

While he grows, Pando is also locked in place. Has been for
tens of thousands of years. Acres of trees, all of them seemingly
different but each connected, tied together in ways no one can
see. That's what makes Pando strong. I want to see the world,
or at least more than Rabbit, but even more than that, I want
to feel rooted. Like no matter what happens, I can face it. That
the next time something terrible happens, I'm strong enough
to get through it without changing everything or leaving it all
behind.

Pando is strong because of his connections. And I don't
know anything about what that would be like.

"Know *what?*" Hayes asks again.

I look at Hayes, at the way his head is tilted toward me, his eyes on my face. His hands are soft at his sides. I say, "I read that when you stand in Pando, the aspen leaves tremble. They're shaped like coins, hanging from the branches. No matter how light the breeze, they all quake. A trembling giant. I'll know what that sounds like. I'll know what it looks like."

Maybe I'll also know what it feels like to be rooted.

"Then you need to see it," Hayes says.

I nod. "I'm going to. When I get there, I'm going to press my back against one of the trees and pretend I'm one of them."

"My mom did that," Hayes says so softly, I find myself not breathing in order to catch his words. "When we were at Big Trees."

"Maybe she wanted to feel strong too?" I whisper.

"I ruined it," Hayes says, his voice gritty now. "I told her to stop embarrassing me." He fists his hands and flicks them open again.

I lick my lips and lower my hands from the plane. "It's finished." *This is it. I did it.* I force air to move steadily in through my nose and out of my mouth, my chest rising so high, I can see it lifting. Regulating breath is vital to regulating heart rate.

I don't bother to turn around when I hear clacking steps moving toward me. "Perfect timing," Nanny Pat says when she stops just behind me. "There's someone I want you to meet."

According to *How to Analyze People: What CIA Spies Know*

but Hope You Never Will, a flaw of human brains is that when we're experiencing emotional turmoil or excitement, our focus narrows. Our minds skip over details, such as a second person's steps. I grimace at my weakness, at not having heard the approach, and then turn.

Beside Nanny Pat is a short, squat man with buzz-cut gray hair, standing with his hands behind his back. He's not in uniform, but just like Nanny Pat, he might as well be. The outlines are crisp enough. His brown eyes are framed with thick black lashes, looking out of place on his lined, tanned face. His mouth is a straight line, and his chin is high as he looks from me to my plane. His bottom lip juts out for a second. "Mind if I . . . ?" Without waiting for a response, he strides toward the ultralight. Hayes backs up, pressed against the wall.

"Gerty," Nanny Pat says, "this is CAP cadet sergeant Ash Hathale."

Focus. Take stock, I order myself. In for a count of three, out for five. In. Out.

"How many hours in the air have you had, Cadet?" His voice is raspy, like his throat is a paper bag his words must push through.

My mind zeroes in on the fact that he called me a cadet even though I haven't joined yet. Like I'm already part of the squadron. "I've had about twenty hours in the air with my grandmother, Sergeant."

Hathale doesn't turn from inspecting the plane. "Unassisted landings and takeoffs?"

"Yes, sir."

He glides his hand along the side of the ultralight. "And you will be turning twelve tomorrow."

It isn't a question, so I don't respond.

Nanny Pat clears her throat. "Gerty understands that while she has the plane now, she will not be permitted to fly it until she has her license."

"But that's four years away," Hathale says. "Why build it now? Who knows if the engine will even turn four years from now?"

"Sir, I built it so I could learn how the plane works and the use of all of its components. If the engine doesn't turn, I'll build a new one."

Hathale faces me, arms crossed. His eyebrows furrow. "No requirements for ultralights. Anyone can fly them. Why are you holding yourself to this standard?"

"I promised Nanny Pat I would."

Hathale stares at me for another long moment. Finally he turns to my grandmother. "You ought to let her have one ride at least, Patty," he says to her. He twists back to me and says, "The thing is, Gerty, until this beast is in the air, it's not a plane. It's an expensive paperweight. You need to fly her, at least once."

Nanny Pat laughs and shakes her head. "Gerty is my rule follower. She respects my conditions. Respects me."

Conditions. The word fills me with shards of ice. They slice as the edges collide. Was the entire build another of Nanny Pat's impossible tests?

"Rule follower? *A pilot?* Those don't go together." Hathale chuckles and pats the side of my plane. "All right, Patty." He tilts his head toward the back of the pole barn. "Let's check out the Cessna. If the Bryce Canyon wildfire creeps this way, we might pull the old girl into play."

"Me or my plane?" Nanny Pat laughs as they head toward the back of the barn.

I sag against the wall next to Hayes. His eyes are wide, the whites showing. What is he panicky about? He didn't just try to impress his future sergeant. "Why are you joining this program?" Hayes whispers.

I finally let loose a grin. "Because someday I'm going to be as scary as him." I turn to my plane. To my paperweight. Is he right? Should I take it for one flight at least? I shake my head. No. I'll be patient. I'll follow Nanny Pat's conditions, and then I'll fly away. I'll go anywhere I want.

Hayes laughs, but it sounds wheezy.

"What?" I snap.

"That look in your eye just now. I think you're already scary."

9

HAYES

I sneak in through the back door after getting home from Nanny Pat's barn. Grandma Louise isn't listening to Chief Skip well; the screen door isn't locked. I hear her singing in the outbuilding, where she's settling the opossums into their crate for the night. Her horse neighs, and in the distance a couple of cows answer.

A husky voice carries through the house from the front porch. "Is that . . . *mooing*?" I recognize it as Jacey. When Charlie turned seven, she leaned into the phone to join Mom singing him "Happy Birthday." Jacey made it like a show tune, her voice going super high and low. She knew to stop exactly as the automated announcer cut in to remind us all that the call was coming from prison, was being recorded, and was running out of time, and then picked up right where she had left off. Calls from prison interrupt like that every three minutes. How many calls would a person have to make to know the timing so well?

Mom laughs. I hear her steps across the living room and into the kitchen, where I'm frozen in the doorway. "Utah and its cows. You get used to it." Her face is like Before Mom, smiling and soft. Then she sees me. Freezes. "Hayes," she says, putting the bowl, empty except for a few popcorn kernels, on the table. "Come on out and meet Jacey in person. She'd love to see—"

"I have homework," I say, and turn down the hall to the room Charlie and I share.

"It's Friday." Jacey is behind Mom now. Based on the big voice and being a firefighter, I expected her to be towering. But Jacey is a small, brown-skinned woman. Her voice is cold, despite the huge smile splitting her face. "I've heard so much about you, Hayes. Nice to finally put a face to the name."

I nod, but any response is clogged in my throat. *What did she hear about me? Mom doesn't know me at all.*

As though reading my mind, Jacey says, her tone warmer now, "Rumor is, you've got a mean football throw." She mimes tossing the ball.

I shake my head. "I stopped playing when I was eight."

"Not too late to pick it back up!"

What does this woman know about me? I feel my breath push from my nose like a bull. "It is when your mom steals jewelry from your coach's wife."

"Hayes," Mom gasps.

Jacey, though, laughs. It sounds like clinking glass. "Stay

angry, little man. But I've got to warn you—it burns up more than it gives."

I stomp down the hall and slam the door.

Late that night I wake to Charlie's soft snores. He still hasn't spoken to me since the fight. Mom tucked him in, kissing his nose and telling him she loved him, that he was "safe as houses" until the morning. It's what she says to him every night. She used to say it to me, too, but the first night she tried after getting out, I rolled onto my side and put the pillow over my ear. Now she says, "Good night, Hayes. I love you." And then she closes the door before I can answer. Or *not* answer.

"Safe as houses" is ridiculous. How are houses safer than anywhere else?

I can't fall back asleep, so I creep to the kitchen for a glass of water. Jacey's rough laugh, coming from the porch outside, stalls me in my tracks. "Of course I brought it!" I hear shuffling, and then the pop and click of a car's trunk opening and closing. "Never leave home without it. Brought *your* old one too, Tara."

Silent as I can, I step out onto the porch. Grandma Louise shoots me a glance, but Mom is focused on whatever Jacey is bringing toward her. It's a tool with a long wooden handle. It looks like an ax, the top painted red, but it juts out on both sides. Opposite the ax is a wedge-shaped blade like a garden hoe.

"Whoa," Mom gasps, and reaches for it. She cradles it on her lap. "Hey there, Polly."

"What's that?" Grandma Louise asks.

I sink down to sit on the porch next to the door. I'm mostly in shadow, but Mom sees me. She grins at me, but I look away.

"A Pulaski," Jacey says. "Hand crews chunk out a fire line, along a road or creek. They'll use these"—she mimes using the wedge side of the tool—"to clear anything that can burn— shrubs, trees, grass, any debris—until the dirt level. Stops the fire in its tracks."

She sits down on the porch step. Mom lowers the Pulaski, running her fingers lightly across the handle. Jacey smiles. "Fire would be raging toward us, so hot that our lungs refused to suck in air, and Tara would be throwing down that line, keeping her crew going."

"Weren't you terrified?" Grandma Louise asks.

Jacey and Mom say "Always" in unison. They grin at each other, an unspoken joke, then Mom sighs. "You've got to understand, I was *constantly* terrified. In prison, out of it, I always felt like I was running from something. At least out there it made sense. I knew what threatened me."

No one speaks, the silence thick and, even from where I perch, awkward. Do they want me out here, listening to this? Do I want to hear it?

Jacey says, "Besides, we knew enough. Like to keep a toe in the black."

"What's that mean?" Grandma Louise asks.

Jacey shrugs. "Charred land can't burn. So long as we could run into the blackened area, we'd be okay. Skin-blistering hot, maybe, but alive." I scrunch my eyebrows, trying to remember how I know this tactic. It was in Mrs. Freid's office. Gerty said if I'm ever in a fire, to find land that's already been scorched.

"Remember that duffer?" Mom asks, her eyes still on the Pulaski.

"Duffer?" Grandma Louise echoes, and I'm glad because I want to know what it means too. "I swear, you have a different language."

Jacey says, "Fir or Douglas trees, their needles on fire, blowing through the air like dandelion puffs from hell, blowing all around you. That's a duffer. The pine cones were blazing, acting like grenades as they rolled down the incline, ready to scorch whatever was in their path." She pauses. "And they would've. If it weren't for Tara's crew."

"You give me too much credit," Mom whispers.

"You don't give yourself enough." Jacey shifts to face Grandma Louise. "Tara hacks out a line, ordering the squad to do the same, but they don't stop at the soil level. No, they manage to dig a legit ditch in minutes, in the middle of a duffer. Those pine cones didn't stand a chance. Probably saved acres. Definitely made life easier for the crew working the line below us."

I try to picture that, Mom saving the forest. For some reason it makes me think of Gerty and how she wants to join CAP to save Pando. Gerty said maybe Mom had leaned against the sequoias so she could pretend to be as strong as them. What if she already was that strong? What if firefighting was what made her realize it?

"How did you know what to do?" Grandma Louise asks.

Mom shrugs. "I had to do what I could. At fire camp—"

"Camp?" I interrupt, even though I'm pretending not to pay attention.

Mom snorts. "I know, makes it sound fun, right? Fire camp is a command center for wildfires. Where all the overhead—the supervisors and other people in charge—and crews live during a fire. We kept mostly separate in our own quarters, but it's basically a temp city for firefighters."

Jacey leans forward. "I met a smoke jumper there. A guy who was so seasoned, he kept steaks wrapped in foil, onions and potatoes diced up with them, in his freezer. Would slip the packet in his lower leg pocket before heading out on a call. Afterward, he'd toss the steak onto the fire, and some lucky fool would have something much better than an MRE."

"Meals ready to eat," Mom cuts in before Grandma can ask.

"Or meals rarely edible, as we called them." Jacey laughs.

"Eh, the meat loaf wasn't *so* bad."

"Anyway," Jacey says, "we all decided Tara should get the steak dinner that night."

"That was a good day." Mom lifts the Pulaski and tucks it under her seat.

"You know what that guy told me?" Jacey says. I lean forward to catch her suddenly hushed words. "He said people either spend one season at camp, or they're there the rest of their lives." She tilts her head toward me. "He nodded to Tara and said, 'That one. She's a lifer. Has fire in her veins.'"

"Mom isn't a firefighter anymore," I say. Jacey's jaw flexes as she narrows her eyes at me.

"Well," Grandma Louise says after too long a pause. "Maybe she once was. But now she's back with us." Grandma plants her hands on the armrests of the rocker and begins to stand. I follow her inside, not wanting to be alone with Mom and Jacey. It feels weird, like I'm a stranger at a birthday party, to be around the two of them. But soon I am back by the living room window, crouched down and peering out to the porch.

I'm not sure what I missed, but neither Mom nor Jacey is smiling anymore. Mom is as still as a statue, her arms crossed. "It's over. There's no path for me." Even in the moonlight I can see the wiry muscles in her arms straining and her jaw clenching. "Not with my record, Jacey."

"You can get it expunged." Jacey is on her feet now. She strides forward and then crouches in front of Mom's chair so they're at the same eye level. "That new law. We can clear your record, get you back into the crew, Tara. Any crew!"

"I already told the captain here. About my record. It wouldn't matter." Mom doesn't look at her.

"Then come back to Cali! You'd be a squad leader in no time.

Think about it! Remember what it's like, really living *life*, saving people, making a difference. Being a hero."

My heart hammers in my chest. Back to California? What about me? What about Charlie?

Mom pushes the rocker back. It screeches across the cement porch. "I deserve that record," she says, and starts to stand. My hands curl and open, curl and open, but the thoughts stick. The memories of our life out there—when she was taking those pills, when they ran out, when Charlie and I were alone more than we weren't—won't budge.

Jacey puts her hand on Mom's shoulder, keeping her in place. "You served your time. It isn't a scarlet letter. You get to move on from it."

Mom shakes her head. "Fire camp can take months. I took enough from my kids. I won't leave them again."

Jacey moves back now as Mom stands. She gets up, tucks her hands in her back pockets and whispers, "So you stay here. Raking yourself over the coals again and again. A different sentence, huh?"

"You don't know what it's like." Now Mom's words are brittle and harsh. Her careful calm shattered for a moment. "We're rebuilding," Tara says. "Charlie and I are good, or at least getting there. Hayes, he's just . . . he's lost so much. He thinks he hates me. Maybe he does." Her chin lifts. "Maybe I deserve it."

Bitterness fills my mouth. Do I hate her? Sometimes, like

when I see her running her hand along the Pulaski again, I do. I really do. But most of the time I simply hate how loving my mom used to be so easy. I hate how much I miss that. I hate that I don't know if it'll ever get better.

"You don't deserve that," Jacey says, her voice firm. "But you do deserve a life, one of your own. You've *earned* it."

I force myself to breathe when my lungs crackle and burn. My heart is ramming against my ribs. She thinks I hate her. Maybe I do. But even more I hate that she'd even think about leaving me again. She didn't have a choice before.

"I can't leave them," Mom whispers. And I realize right away what she didn't say. She didn't say she doesn't *want* to leave us.

"I see you with those boys, Tara," Jacey whispers. "They don't have you now." She bends and picks up the Pulaski, then holds it out to Mom handle first. "I stopped at a forester station on the way up here. There's a fire, calling it the Bryce Canyon, heading north toward Fishlake. I'm going there tomorrow. They need more hands. I'll put in a good word for you."

Mom takes the Pulaski as my heart leaps into my throat. But then she lowers it to the porch. "I don't think so, Jacey."

The smaller woman seems to loom over Mom. She lets out a long breath. "Think about it. You want to be here for those boys? First you've got to show up for yourself." She snorts. "Keep one toe in your own black."

10

GERTY

Before I even open my eyes the next morning, I decide.

I'm going to tell Alex and Jennifer about the airplane today. Then I'll break it to them about CAP. It'll be fine. I bet they'll even be proud of me for building the plane. Maybe they'll put me in charge of building more things around the property.

It's chilly when I wake, the house still dark and the pine plank floor so cold, my toes curl as I push my feet into my slippers to start the morning chores.

The whole house is quiet. Lilith must've slept through the night, because the fire in the woodstove has burned out. I peek in my sister's crib and watch her chest rise and fall. Alex and Jennifer's bed is right beside the crib, and Jennifer's arm is to the side, like she fell asleep with her hand on Lilith. Even though it's only early September, the nights are cold in our woods, so we usually keep the stove on a low burn overnight.

I go to the woodpile stacked beside the house and bring in an armful of logs. My toes are freezing from the cold dew, and I have to juggle the logs while kicking off my damp slippers on the rag rug inside the door. I stack the wood inside the stove. The embers are out, which is no good at all. I sigh and nest a bunch of smaller, dryer pieces of kindling under the logs. Smoke curls out around me, and I know if it were a school day, I'd be in for Jaxson complaining that "someone smells like a campfire."

Next, I grab the blue enamel percolator from the counter and fill it with coffee grounds and then water. The tap is running on a drizzle, which also is no good at all. Alex is going to be in a bad mood about that. He's always thinking about water. Sometimes I think Alex's whole brain is a lake, sloshing from one thought to another. We have a water tower he made from plastic barrels. He fills other barrels at the community well, drags them back to our house in a trailer pulled by his four-wheeler, and then dumps them into the water tanks. It takes all weekend. The tanks are connected to a bunch of tubes. He says they're gravity fed. I think they're not eating nearly enough gravity, because some days they just plain don't work. There's a full bucket beside the sink, and I consider using that water instead for the coffee, even though I know Jennifer pulled it from the water lines in the canals she and Alex dug from the house to the stream in the woods. It's for washing and flush-ing toilets, not for drinking. The coffee is boiling hot, though, right? I could add some iodine. . . . No, I can't do that.

I sigh and wait out the dribbling faucet to fill the pot. I've got to show my parents I *am* independent and smart if they're ever going to let me fly that plane.

I realize then what would really make a difference, what would truly show them that I'm practically an adult. I could start the generator.

During the night, if we need any electricity—like when I had pneumonia and we had to run a humidifier as I slept—we get power from a few golf cart batteries Alex rigged together. But during the day all our power comes from the generator. It's Saturday, so Jennifer will be spending the day on laundry and meal prep for the week, which means the kitchen needs to be bright and buzzing.

I've watched Alex turn on the generator lots of times, but I've never done it by myself. The generator is the most expensive thing we own. When it didn't start a few months ago, Alex lost a whole day of roofing work in town because he had to go back and forth from the library, YouTubing ways to repair it, and I had to go to school the next day with my pants still damp because the washing didn't have time to dry on the line. If Alex knew he could depend on me to help with the generator, then

I know he'd be much more likely to hear me out on the CAP and airplane secrets. He goes into town all the time for supplies and work. Once he learns about the airplane, maybe he'll even put me in charge of the generator!

Donald the rooster screeches as I shove my feet into Alex's boots. Mine are right next to his, but I'd have to untie them and then lace them back up, and I'm eager to get started proving myself. Alex's feet are a lot bigger than mine, but I'm just going a few yards to where the generator, a big black-and-silver boxlike machine, stands beside the house, so I'll deal with the floppy steps. "Not now, Donald," I snap at the rooster. He fluffs up his feathers but runs off into the trees instead of chasing me. I yank the full gas can out from under the tarp where Alex keeps it and other yard tools, then trudge toward the generator. I twist off the cap at the top as I walk. A whistle and rustling come from the woods. Donald, I guess, is telling me off chicken-style.

"I don't like you, either!" I mutter as I carry the gas can, holding it tight against my chest. Alex must've filled it on his trip into town yesterday, because it's super heavy and full. I hear the fuel sloshing in the can.

A twig snaps behind me, too loudly for it to have been Donald. I startle and gasoline splashes onto my shirt and up to my chin. The smell, sharp and painful, makes me gasp. "Ah, that's not nice," says a high-pitched voice. "We haven't even met yet!"

Between the spilled gasoline and the stranger, I'm startled. That's not even right. I'm weak. All I know is narrowed to two things—spilled fuel and a stranger—and both of those are *bad*. My dull human instincts take over. I step backward, still sucking in gasoline-tinged air, and trip when the heel of Alex's too-big boot hits the edge of the generator. I land, hard, on my tailbone, my legs in the air against the generator, gasoline covering all of me and it. The rusty edge of the can somehow scraped my arm, just above the elbow, and a bead of blood blooms.

From the shadows edging the woods steps a tall, scraggly man with bright red hair. Half his mouth is pulled back in a mocking smile as though pulled by a fishhook. His eyes are cold as they sweep over me, weak and on the ground. My heart hammers in my chest, cataloging my mistakes—wearing too-big boots, not telling anyone what I was doing, being unaware of my surroundings, and, worst of all, spilling fuel all over the generator and myself.

The man, though, is seemingly as calm as can be, the air going in and out of his crooked nose like a teakettle about to boil. Slowly, so slowly, he pulls a pack of cigarettes from his back pocket. Standing just a few feet from me, he shakes one out and slips it into his mouth. He winks as he then pulls out a match. I want to scream at him to stop—he's too close to me, to the generator, to the spilled fuel, my sleeping family—but nothing comes out of my mouth. I can't breathe, can't hear him, can't do anything but sit there, sprawled on the ground, my crowded brain suddenly empty of anything but panic.

"Step away from my daughter." Alex. I don't see him, didn't even hear him approach, but suddenly he's there. My dad is tall, with coiled muscle, a bushy brown beard, and shaggy hair. He's wearing an unbuttoned flannel shirt and jeans. No shoes. They're the clothes he wore last night; he must've thrown them on and run out, somehow knowing from inside the house that something was wrong and that I was too soft to notice, despite being in the thick of it.

My eyes slide back to the man, whose snort comes out again as a whistle. He rolls the cigarette around his mouth, then pulls it down with a cupped hand and half a smile. "Didn't mean to startle the little lady," the man says. "Name's . . . Waylan." The man's mouth twitches as he says the fake name. "Yeah. Waylan. Let's go with that."

"What are you doing on our land, *Waylan*?" Alex grabs me by the elbow, his thumb brushing the scrape, and yanks me to my feet. My arm barks in protest. Alex's nose scrunches as he takes in the smell, and his eyes flick to the gas can, still on its side, gas falling from the top in slow glugs. I lunge to grab it, but Alex's grip on my elbow tightens. I still. Slowly he rights the can with his bare foot.

The whole time the man stands in front of us. I'm too shaken at first to notice the tells that he's not as casual as he appears to be. It's the way his fingers flex at his side. The way his pulse hammers in his neck. His bottom lip juts out. "I didn't think anyone lived out this way, so deep in the woods." The man turns his head as though taking in the wilderness around us. "Not one for neighbors?"

"Not particularly." Alex shifts so he's squarely in front of me. I smell the pine soap he uses and feel the soft flannel of his shirt against my cheek. "Seems you've lost your way, Waylan. How about I walk you back to the road while my daughter gets herself cleaned up."

"Oh, now that's not necessary," the man says, that whistling sound again escaping his nose.

Alex straightens. "I insist." Without looking away from Waylan, he grabs my shoulder, turning me back to the house. I'm not sure my body will listen when I tell it to move, but it does. I back away from them. "These woods are dangerous if you don't know the way," Alex says. I don't think Alex is talking about the bobcats and bears.

"Gerty, my shoes," Alex says without taking his eyes off the stranger. I kick them off and he slides his bare feet inside.

My father moves forward deliberately, swiftly, and it terrifies me. This is how Alex's body shifted that time we saw a cougar in the woods. This is how he trained us to act when we're in danger. Another memory tugs at me, of Alex back when I was a silly kindergartner and we lived in a house with a yard and neighbors and a car parked in the driveway. Back when I called Alex "Daddy."

I remember sitting on a rug with dolls all around me when he barged through the door with the same forced calm and clenched jaw. He strode toward Jennifer ("Mommy" then) and said something about how, on top of the thing that had happened a few weeks before—the one we don't talk about—there had been a shooting in his office that day. He said we had to act, that we couldn't wait, that the world wasn't safe for us, that we were too soft. He said we were in danger if we stayed. I remember hearing him say we couldn't stay, and it made sense to me that the world wasn't safe, that it was out to get us. After all, only a few weeks before the shooting, everything had shifted right in our own house when Matthew . . .

I slam the door on the memory of what first splintered our world and turned it jagged, the moment that none of us talk about and never acknowledge. The shooting was what prompted Alex to decide we had to leave. But sometimes I think we really left everything behind to shake Matthew's ghost.

Now we're in danger again because I was soft. "Get inside, Gerty," Alex says as these memories rattle and kick inside my mind.

I sprint across the wet dirt. The door swings open and Jennifer's hand darts out, then yanks me inside and shuts the door. She pushes me behind her. "Mommy," I whisper. For just a moment she becomes soft too, pulling me into her side.

"Tell me again," Alex says an hour later.

My scrubbed-clean hair is wrapped in a towel, and I'm in my last clean outfit, my sweatshirt hood pulled up like a hug around my ears. The washing is going to have to wait another few days. There is too much gasoline on and around the generator to start it. Alex used what was left of our dribbling water supply after my long, long shower to clean the ground around where I spilled the fuel.

"Focus. Take stock. Always be aware of surroundings. Listen. React. And make sure someone knows where you are and what you're doing."

"And?"

"Leave the generator alone," I add, dropping the bad words he has been using all morning when listing that rule.

"What were you thinking, Gerty?" Alex snarls. "Even if that man hadn't been lurking in the woods, your actions put us all in danger. We depend on that generator!"

Jennifer clears her throat behind Alex. "But if Gerty hadn't been there, we wouldn't have known he was around."

Alex stiffens. He doesn't like when my mom contradicts him. "*I* knew something was wrong. I would've found him."

"No, you knew Gerty left the percolator going."

Alex spears Jennifer with a glare. Lilith whimpers, and Jennifer shifts so that the carrier goes from her back to her front.

My little sister rests her head against Jennifer's chest, listening to her heartbeat.

"Why can't I call you Dad anymore?" The words are out of my mouth before I know I'm speaking them. Another broken rule: action without consideration.

Alex's jaw flexes and his eyes narrow. "You know why."

"I don't," I say, and this time the edge to my voice is intentional.

His nostrils flare. He's fighting to stay calm; I know because he taught me how to do the same. He backs up, arms crossed, eyes to the window, focusing on the distance. "We decided it's better for you to be independent. To know you need to count on yourself. That you're as important in this family as anyone else."

"But I'm not." My bottom lip shakes, and I bite down hard to steady it, take a breath and continue. "*You* decided one day that I shouldn't call you Dad. Like you decided that we shouldn't live in town anymore. Or spend Christmas with Nanny Pat or even celebrate it at all. And *you* decided it was better to have generators and buckets of water and woodstoves and—"

"It's my job to keep us safe!" Alex yells, his control slipping. Alex's control *never* slips. Lilith whimpers again, and Jennifer, eyes wide, pats her bottom, taking a couple of shuffling steps backward as she does.

"I miss him too," I whisper. The words are tissue thin, barely there, but they hit my parents like shrapnel. Both flinch. Neither speaks. I've already broken so many rules; now I've defied the biggest one: don't talk about what happened before; don't remember; don't mourn.

Alex shudders. Then he juts a finger toward me. "Pack your stuff." He turns to Jennifer. "You too. Pack everything. That man was scouting. I'm sure of it. He probably has a crew. They're either laying low between jobs and think this is where they can camp, or they're going to rob us. We aren't safe here."

Jennifer's gaze darts to me and down to Lilith. Her voice shaking, she says, "You said we'd wait for Gerty to finish the school year before we move. Give her this time to—"

"That was before *this*," Alex says. "It's time to go to Oregon, like we talked about. The land outside Portland that my father bought. We know enough now. We can do it right. There's a well on the property. A trailer we can live in until we can build something sturdier. A pond. Some time away from everything will set us right again, get fool ideas out of Gerty's head."

"No," I whisper. I know he hears me, but he doesn't answer.

"We'll leave as soon as we can," Alex says. "I'm getting supplies."

"No," I say again, but no one reacts.

"We're getting out of here," Alex says. "That man, the wildfire, they're red flags. We're leaving."

"No!" I shout. Pando has lived through countless wildfires.

Alex's nostrils flare. His jaw clenches. His arms bow slightly outward as he turns toward me. Fury. These are signs of fury. "I said we're going, Gerty! We're not taking chances. We're leaving! And you will call me by my name. Understood?" Before I can answer, he stomps from the room.

"Mom," I whisper.

Jennifer shakes her head and then buries her face in Lilith's neck. "Listen to Alex." Another impossible condition: be independent, think for yourself, rely on yourself, but listen to Alex, listen to Jennifer, listen to Nanny Pat, follow the rules.

Maybe I'm tired of following rules.

Maybe I'm tired of being a paperweight.

11

HAYES

Jacey's voice wakes me. "Come along. You don't have to stay. You don't have to say anything at all. Remember, we're on the outs now. You can go places, Tara, just because you want to, and the worst thing that happens is someone tells you to leave."

I open my eyes, the smell of coffee hitting me at the same time as Jacey's words, both trickling in from the kitchen. Charlie is sitting cross-legged on his bed, face smeared with the innards of a jelly doughnut. I groan and look at my phone. I slept in later than I usually do, even for a Saturday morning. It's already that weird zone between being too late for breakfast and too early for lunch. I hope there are more doughnuts for me.

"Hey," I say to him as I pull on some clothes. He pretends not to hear me. His eye is now the same grape color as the jelly. I tie on my sneakers. Grandma is bending the no-shoes-in-the-house rule because of the opossum babies. They're not exactly potty-trained. Better safe than sorry. "Are there any more doughnuts?"

He pushes up from the bed, leaving purple streaks on the sheets from his fingers, and stomps down the hall.

I sigh and rub at my eyes. I had the same dream last night, of running toward fire only to have it creep farther away. *It's Jacey's fault*, I think as I hear her voice again, this time asking Grandma Louise if there's any cream for her coffee. I hate Jacey.

But I love doughnuts.

I'm going to grab a doughnut, first one I see, even if it's glazed, and head back to my room. Charlie already broke Grandma Louise's strict no-eating-in-your-room rule (started mostly so the opossums don't start sleeping under our beds with the crumbs), but I'll be so fast, she won't even notice. In and out.

"What's the point?" I hear Mom ask. I'm at the doorway now and can see into the kitchen. Mom's hair is down, hanging to her waist in thick waves. Her face is scrubbed clean, but there are dark circles under her eyes. Maybe she had bad dreams too.

"See if it sparks any interest," Jacey says with a grin.

"Terrible pun." Mom rolls her eyes. "Fine, I'll go. But I'm not sticking around."

"*Yes!*" Jacey says, and slurps her coffee.

"Go where?" As soon as the words are out of my mouth, I

wish I could gulp them back in. Mom, Jacey, and Grandma Louise startle, one of the baby opossums on Grandma Louise's shoulder opening its mouth in a gaping hiss. So much for my in-and-out plan.

"To fire camp," Jacey says when no one else answers. "A spike is setting up south of here, in case winds change."

With those words, I swear I hear that ocean of fire roaring in my ears. "No," I say. The room blurs in front of me. My hip hits the table, knocking over a chair. "You can't go. You can't."

Mom's jaw clenches, and then she's in front of me, her hands cold on my cheeks. "I'm right here," she says.

I shake my head to make her hands fall. Grandma Louise is hovering behind Mom, her eyes wet. In the doorway, though, is Charlie, a grin splitting his face. "You're going to fight that fire, Mom? You're going to save people?"

Jacey's chin pops into the air. "Your mom is the coolest, isn't she, kiddo?"

"You can't go," I say again. "They won't let you."

Mom stands and holds her elbows. "I'm going to drop off Jacey. Maybe talk to a captain there, see if what she said about expunging my record is even possible."

I shake my head again. I realize I dropped the doughnut. One of the opossums is nibbling on it at my feet. "They won't let you. They'll see you're a criminal and they—"

Mom rears back like I slapped her. Charlie pushes in front of her. "I hate you," he yells at me. "I hate you so much!"

I can't breathe. Because in that moment I hate him, too. I hate how he brags about her being a firefighter, even though it was while in prison. I hate how he smiles and has friends and forgets. I hate how he forgives.

"Hayes!" Mom calls, but I'm already running. I can't be there, standing in the kitchen eating doughnuts, talking about her leaving again. Talking about her going into fire. I can't. I can't. I can't breathe. Ican'tbreathe. Ican't—

I trip running from the porch, slamming to my knees. Twisting, I see what snared my shoelace: the Pulaski. I grab it, holding it across my chest, and take off. Maybe it doesn't make sense, but if Mom can't find the Pulaski, maybe she won't go. Maybe she'll stay.

Because here's the thing. During those years when Mom was gone, she wasn't the only one who was scared. I was *always* scared too.

I spend the next few hours walking in the woods, wishing I had eaten that doughnut. And then I find myself standing at the entrance to Nanny Pat's barn. I realize two things: I'm still grasping the Pulaski, and I don't even know if Gerty will be here. She finished the plane the day before. Maybe she's off joining CAP and making cool soon-to-be pilot friends.

A truck rumbles down the road toward the barn, kicking up dust and going way too fast. A hand thrusts out from the shadows of the barn and encircles my upper arm. "Get in here. *Now*," Gerty whispers as she yanks me toward her.

Gerty's hand slides from my arm to cover my mouth. "*Shh!*"

I nod and she drops her hand. We press against the inside of the door as the truck screeches to a stop. I lean the Pulaski against the wall and follow Gerty toward a small window. We peek out the side.

A man in a flannel shirt and faded jeans hops from the still-running truck. He's walking so fast that he's nearly running, his fisted hands covered in dirt. Mud is smudged across his forehead, too, as though he smeared it there while wiping his brow. "*Pat!*" he yells. "Patricia, I need to talk to you right now!"

Nanny Pat's door opens. She looks totally calm, white button-down shirt pressed and navy slacks crisp, her face smooth as she walks toward him. "To what do I owe the pleasure, Alex?"

Alex? This is Gerty's dad? I poke her side, but she doesn't look away from the window.

"What did you do with the money?"

Nanny Pat raises her chin. "What money?" Her words are crisp.

"The money I buried in the woods. Almost all of it is gone!"

Nanny Pat's eyes flick to the barn for a moment. Both Gerty and I pull back from the window. Gerty's breathing fast, her shoulders rising and falling. I peek again out the glass.

"I assure you, I have no idea what you're talking about," Nanny Pat says. "But perhaps you should've considered a bank. Maybe an animal found your cache."

Alex crosses his arms. "Jennifer didn't tell you about the money?"

"No. My daughter hasn't spoken to me in more than a year." Nanny Pat holds her hands behind her back, rocking on her heels. "Might I assume you're in need of funds?"

"Not from you," Alex snaps. Then he stills. "Gerty. You don't think she'd—"

"What use would an eleven-year-old have for money?" Nanny Pat asks. Beside me, Gerty sags a little, her mouth opening in a circle as she finally breathes out. Nanny Pat continues, "What's going on? You seem harried."

"We're leaving," Alex says. "The lot of us. The money's a setback, but we'll get by." He rubs the back of his neck.

Nanny Pat stiffens. "You're leaving."

Alex nods. "Tonight. Tomorrow first thing at the latest."

"I'm supposed to head to the CAP headquarters in Cedar City this afternoon, figure out how to be of aid if the Bryce Canyon wildfire heads north." For the first time Nanny Pat doesn't seem collected. She's leaning toward Alex. "I'd like to say goodbye to Gerty, Jennifer, meet the baby." Her voice hitches on the word *baby*.

Alex pauses, staring at her for a beat too long. Finally he

says, "Gerty ran off this morning, I imagine to let all her school friends know. The rest of it, that's Jennifer's decision."

"I'll be gone tonight," Nanny Pat says. "Where are you headed? How will I stay in touch with you?"

Alex looks away. "Jennifer knows how to reach you."

Nanny Pat slowly closes her eyes. When she opens them, Alex is striding back to the truck. "Wait!" she calls. Alex pauses, not turning around. "Gerty! She could stay with me. Finish school. I'll make sure she has everything she needs."

Alex keeps walking.

"Did you ask her," Nanny Pat calls out, "if she wants to go? Did you even ask?" She stands there, as still as a statue, as Alex gets into the truck, turns it around in three quick movements, and drives back down the driveway.

Next to me, Gerty is just as still. Me? I'm shaking all over, so hard that I swear I'm going to knock over the buckets and tools surrounding me. I know what that's like, to have grown-ups steal your choices, decide what happens next without giving you a vote. How everything can change with one decision. I swear, Alex's footsteps back to his truck sounded like a gavel slamming down.

Slowly Gerty raises her finger to her mouth. I peek again. Nanny Pat smooths her palms along her pants. Nods once and then turns on her heel toward the pole barn. "She's coming!" I hiss to Gerty.

But Gerty slowly shakes her head, again pressing her finger

to her lips, and I see Nanny Pat isn't coming into the barn after all. Instead she gets into her SUV parked out front. Soon she also disappears down the driveway.

"She covered for me," Gerty says. "She must've known I stole the money for the plane from Dad—I mean, Alex. But she covered for me." Her eyes flash to the ultralight, assembled in front of the garage doors.

"What did your dad mean, about you leaving?"

"Why are you here?" Gerty asks instead. "And why did you bring a Pulaski?"

Figures Gerty would know what it is, but it's annoying anyway. "My mom, it was hers. Her friend says the wildfire might head this way."

Gerty watches me for a second. Then she strides across the barn to a cluttered workbench. She opens a drawer and pulls out a plastic water bottle and a couple granola bars, which she thrusts at me. "You look peaked."

I grunt thanks and tear into the snacks. "Tell me what your dad meant," I say between bites. "You're leaving?"

Gerty steps toward the plane. I don't think she fully heard me. She pulls off her sweatshirt, tying it around her waist, and I see her arm is scratched, a bruise blooming around the cut just above her elbow. "I wish I could've seen him, just once. This time of year he'll be green. But in a month? A bright yellow. All the aspen clones, they change color at once. That's how you know they're all rooted in Pando." She presses her forehead against the windshield. "I wish I could've flown there." She hums something, and I realize she's singing "Happy Birthday."

Something stirs inside me, too large to crumple and throw away. It's anger, rippling from my heart to flood and fill me. I rub my knuckles against my chest, trying to keep it from erupting. Parents shouldn't be able to change everything. They shouldn't leave.

"Then do it," I say. The words are like flint, and the angry monster inside me is suddenly made of flames.

"What?" Gerty says. I think it's the first time I've ever surprised her.

I wonder what she sees when she looks at me, struggling to breathe around the anger inside me, the monster that *is* me. I swallow some of the water and then say it again. "Do it. You know how to fly. You know everything about the plane. So let's go. Fly over Pando. See it. And then we come back, and we do what they tell us. We'll follow their rules, even when they're wrong or they don't make sense. But first? We do this for us."

Gerty straightens. "They wouldn't even know we left. It'd only take an hour." She jerks her chin toward me. "When we get back, I'll say goodbye to Nanny Pat." She doesn't add "and you." She doesn't have to; I hear it.

"Or you could say goodbye to Alex and Jennifer," I whisper. She swallows.

Something cracks amid the churning in my chest, dousing the monster, as Gerty strides back over to the workbench on the far side of the barn and picks up a matte black helmet, then snaps it in place on her head.

Everything that's crowded my mind—worries about Mom and Charlie, about how quickly everything changes, about where I belong, *if* I belong—all of it fades away with the snaps of Gerty's helmet. Maybe that's what's been wrong with me for so long, the reason I had to have lunches with Mrs. Freid. Maybe I felt *too* much. Now? I feel only one thing. That I want to do this. That I want to see Gerty's face as she flies, when *she* is the one in control instead of her parents or her grandma or anyone else. Maybe I couldn't stop Mom from uprooting everything in my life, but I can be there when Gerty gets at least this—seeing her trees—before her dad does the same to her.

And maybe I need to see her trees too. Maybe seeing Pando will finally claw away the pasted-on image of the Mother of the Forest in my head. Maybe Pando could also be *mine*. Pando's trees aren't scarred, they aren't horrible, they aren't alone; they're green, all of them. They're strong.

There's a second helmet on the workbench. It's larger and steely blue. I think it must be Nanny Pat's.

Gerty doesn't move as I stride to her side and then buckle the helmet strap under my chin. Something flickers across her face for just a second, and then she lifts her chin. "I might crash. You should know your pilot's history before getting into a plane," Gerty says. "And I haven't flown by myself before."

For some reason the unsteadiness in her voice makes me braver. It's like we switch roles for a second. So I grab Mom's Pulaski. "Let's go."

12

GERTY

About an hour later, Hayes yanks open the garage door in front of the plane. Nanny Pat's long, flat driveway will make a perfect runway; the plane is so light and slow that it should need only about 350 feet of space to take off and land.

Hayes had been ready to jump into the plane right away, but I forced both of us to stop. We ate a couple more granola bars as I studied the map hanging over the workbench. I gave Hayes time to reconsider.

But he didn't. And neither have I.

I force a long, deep breath and count the exhale to make sure it's longer than the inhale. If I soak my brain in oxygen, maybe it'll stop telling my heart that we should panic. *Focus. Take stock.* A pilot needs to stay calm. I'm not worried about my plane; I know I built it right. I'm not worried about flying, either; I know I can fly. But I'm breaking a lot of rules, and if we get caught, I don't know what Alex or Nanny Pat will do. I don't like not knowing. *So don't get caught,* I tell myself. One hour, there and back, and no one will ever know but us.

I grab the clipboard from the workbench. Every flight must start with a walk-around. Nanny Pat says even pilots with thousands of hours in the air fall victim to carelessness. Not me. I'm not reckless.

Except for the whole about-to-fly-without-a-license-when-no-one-else-knows-and-also-bringing-a-passenger-in-a-one-person-plane decision.

Quickly I run through the list, checking all 281 inches of wingspan. I make sure the gas tank has a full five gallons. I check the fuselage, the fixed-pitch wood propeller. I make sure latches close and that the safety harness is secured to the woven canvas seat. "C'mon," I say to Hayes. His face is set and jaw clenched. I nab the Pulaski from his hand and use bungee cords to strap it to the back of the seat. He sits in the seat, sweat beading on his forehead, the only sign that he's nervous. His hands aren't even curling, simply lying flat on his legs.

I take a big breath. *What are you doing, Gerty?* I ask myself. It comes out in my dad's voice. That, for some reason, makes me run to the back of the pole barn, where I pull Nanny Pat's emergency kit from under the seat of the Cessna. It has straps like a backpack, so I loop it over my shoulders.

Hayes scoots to the side of the wide seat when I peak an

eyebrow at him. I am *not* sitting on his lap. I know the responsible thing to do would be to tell him not to come along, that wanting him there beside me even though he'll be as useful as a lump is one of many things making me soft. But I don't say anything.

I turn on the engine, and it picks up immediately. Temperature gauge tells me it's seventy-two degrees. I push the little button beneath it to turn on the stopwatch. One hour. That's all I'm going to give myself. That's all a first run should be anyway. The airspeed indicator is beside the temperature gauge. I tap it with my finger. "We'll stay in the green range," I tell Hayes. "If it goes to the yellow or the red, let me know." I don't need him to keep an eye on this, but I want him to feel like he has a job. Tasks sometimes yank people out of panic, and I don't know what kind of passenger he's going to be.

The altitude indicator is the next control. Blue is for sky. Brown is for ground. I've got to keep the airspeed indicator in the green and the altitude indicator blue. The vertical speed and the directional gyro will help me stay aligned with where I need to be. The fuel gauge is up to full. The turn coordinator will help me avoid stalling the engine. One swoop over Pando, back to Nanny Pat's. No problem.

I reach over Hayes and pull the safety harness across us both, clicking it into place. Then I grab the gear shift and we're moving forward.

The most dangerous times in a flight are the takeoff and landing. "Don't move," I order Hayes when he leans forward to watch the temperature gauge.

The plane isn't fast—that's not the way it's built. It bounces a bit as it rumbles ahead. I think of what Nanny Pat told me the first time she let me take the controls of her plane. "You've got to believe you can do it. Otherwise, you'll spend all your life on the ground." I'm done being a paperweight. I can do this. I *am* doing this.

"What did you say?" Hayes hisses in my ear.

I ignore him. I'm hovering just over brown sliding into the blue. Then, blue, blue, blue. Hands steady, I pull on the stick. We're easing upward. Soon we're tilted so I don't see the ground at all. Just sky. My lungs deflate as I ease the stick forward.

"Is it supposed to be this loud?" Hayes yells into my ear.

I roll my eyes. We're in a plane without doors that runs with a Volkswagen engine. Yeah, it's supposed to be loud. He shifts closer to me. Maybe it's the no-door thing, or the wind, or the reality that this is *happening*, but I shiver. We're in the sky!

Hayes hoots, a grin shining on his face. He was so angry on the ground, but it's like he left that all behind and now is something else. I think maybe he's proud of me, of us.

And suddenly we're laughing, and it feels like my heart is hovering outside my body, like it's dancing.

Hayes lifts his hand, making it wave in the burst of cool air flowing around us. "You did it!" he cheers.

I show off a little, making us rise and fall with his hand, and he laughs even harder. The sky is so blue and endless.

I spot smoke in the distance—the Bryce Canyon wildfire Hayes said was approaching. It's closer than I thought it would be. I don't know how fast fire moves, but I didn't think it'd be close enough to spot the smoke.

While Hayes hoots and points out trees and mountains beside me, I keep an eye on the directional gyro. We put the plume of gray behind us. We're moving past the flat tundra toward Fishlake's mountains. "This is amazing," Hayes shouts, leaning out the side to look at the ground below us. "*You're* amazing!"

I bite my lip to keep my smile from splitting my face. *This is the best birthday I've ever had,* I think as the trees below us shrink to broccoli. I make my worries do the same—shrink, shrink, shrink. There is only now: the sky above me, the friend beside me, and the wind tugging away any other thought.

The few cars we pass look like toys running along tracks, and Hayes has fully forgotten to be afraid. Then, no roads are below us anymore as we soar over mountains. Sage and juniper disappear into watercolor smudges. "Whoa," Hayes says.

I grin and Hayes smiles back. *We're doing this!* We're actually doing this. We soar over another ridge. I bring us down lower, dipping into the valley between two mountainsides. When I pull us back upward, I spot a glimmer of blue in the far distance—the lake. Pando spreads outward from the lake,

I know, in acres of tentacle-like stretches of aspen. I lean forward when I see a flash of green. That's him! I pull the stick, picking up speed.

"Gerty!" Hayes screams.

A bird slams into the cockpit through the open doorway. Its black body thumps against the windshield. I twist from it, the plane dropping too quickly, as Hayes bellows again. My hands and the gear stick are one, cemented together in fear. What am I supposed to do? *Focus, Gerty! Take stock.*

For a moment everything quiets. All I hear is the rush of wind in my ears. Even the engine must be holding its breath. The engine! We stalled.

And then? A high, keening sound rocks through me. Hayes. He's screaming, his mouth an open cave. And the side of the mountain is where the sky ought to be.

Yet my voice is steady when I shout, "Hold on!"

His arms wrap around my waist. I cover his hands with mine as everything I built shatters around us.

The ground is so hard, and I am too soft.

13

HAYES

I don't see anything, and it takes me way too long to realize that it's because my eyes are closed. The air around me isn't as cold as it was moments before. It's not slamming against my face. I open my eyes and try to get my bearings. The safety harness is cutting into my shoulder and my waist. Something snapped when the plane hit the ground. The wing? The fuselage bounces once. We're teetering—the ground below me, the sky beside Gerty. I squeeze my eyes shut as something cracks and we slam down. Teeter again.

Everything stops. *Am I dead?* The side of my face is pressed against something hard and cold. Slowly I open my eyes again.

I gasp. The sky is a light blue. How can it still be day? How can the sun still be shining? We *crashed*.

My chest rises and falls, rises and falls. The fuselage

shifts again, an eerie moaning rumbling below me as the rods holding the structure together bend.

A groan.

Gerty! I'm hanging from the seat belt, and she is wedged below me, my cheek smooshed into the side of her helmet. I lick my lip. It's sticky and wet with blood and gaping where my tooth sank into it when we crashed. I try to call Gerty's name, but my voice comes out in a croak. My arms are still clasped around her waist. I try to slide my hand out from under her, and the groan turns to a whimper. "Gerty?" I whisper. She doesn't move.

We have to get out of the plane. I don't know a lot about airplanes, but in movies they tend to blow up. Are we going to blow up? Slowly I try again to slip my hand out from under Gerty, and her whole body shudders when my arm comes free. I fumble to find the clasp on the safety harness, and have to hold back a scream when I see my hand. It's covered in blood, as though I sank my arm into a bucket of red paint. I flex and curl my fingers. Nothing hurts. I twist my arm. It's stiff and probably going to be bruised, but none of the pain is sharp. It's not my blood.

"Gerty?" I whisper again. She doesn't answer but her breath turns raspy. "Gerty, I'm going to unlock the seat belt. I think . . . I think I'm going to fall onto you. I'll try to catch us, but you should be ready, okay?"

She doesn't answer. I swallow, my mouth gritty and dry,

then press the button. We fall in a thud. I yank Gerty toward me and twist, trying to take the brunt of the impact away from her arm, but we still land hard and Gerty is still below me. She yelps, and the sound hollows my chest.

I hoist her so we're both standing upright, inside the cockpit of the plane. "We need to get out of here," I say. Only then do I really look at Gerty. Her right arm is cradled against her ribs. Blood drips from her bent elbow, and something white is jutting out of it, right over the spot that was scraped earlier today. *Please don't be a bone.* Her green eyes seem too large for her pale, narrow face. Like me, she must've bitten her lip on impact, because it's split down the middle and bleeding. In that moment she doesn't look fierce. She looks like a little girl. "Are you okay, Gerty?" I whisper as my legs shake. Standing is taking too much force, like the crash rattled my bones into soup.

Gerty grits her teeth. Her face stiffens. She swallows. Suddenly she's scurrying up the sideways seat and through the open doorway. She lands on the other side of the fuselage. "C'mon, Hayes. We've got work to do."

14

GERTY

Are you okay, Gerty?"

What a soft question.

There's a piece of metal stuck in my arm. My plane just crashed. No one knows where we are. We have no food, no water, and no cell phone reception, and it's going to be dark in a few hours. I don't bother answering him.

Though I landed on my feet outside the ultralight, the flare of pain in my arm shoots through me and nearly buckles my knees. I know what caused the injury—the loose hinge, the one that had only one screw. The one I thought wouldn't make a difference. The screw must've fallen out in the crash, and now the hinge is in my arm. And I know it isn't large, maybe the span of a quarter. But it's wedged into my skin, right above my already-cut elbow, and it feels like an ax blade.

Hayes lands like a boulder beside me. My head is

foggy; I didn't even hear him climbing the seat. I unsnap the helmet and sit cross-legged beside the wreckage.

"Shouldn't we get away from the plane?" asks Hayes, his voice reedy and thin. He's holding his phone, the screen cracked across the front. Even if it weren't broken beyond repair, there's no reception here. "Isn't it gonna blow up or something?"

I roll my eyes. "That only happens in movies. There's maybe three gallons of gas total in there."

"Well, I don't know!" Hayes says, and it's almost a sob. "I don't know anything."

Alex's voice travels along my spine, steeling each bone until I'm standing again. *Focus. Take stock. Always be aware of surroundings. Listen. React.* "I know lots. And I'm getting us out of here."

When we left our clean little house with a yard and a garage, for a few days we lived in a tent on the plot of land that would become our new home. Nanny Pat had given Jennifer the land as a wedding gift, maybe to develop it someday. But my parents never touched it, letting the woods grow thick. Alex said it was too close to Nanny Pat and too accessible to the rest of the world, but it would work for the time being, until we learned how to make do entirely on our own. He spent most of those first few days away, meeting with banks and buying supplies and going to the library to research.

But Mom, I mean, *Jennifer* and I, we stayed in the woods.

At night Alex would build a big fire and teach us the rules that would keep us safe. He told us about the camp he had been sent to when he got into some trouble when he was a teenager, and how a guide had led him and some other kids on a hike into the mountains and back again. He told us about cougars and bears and snakes. Plants that would fill our throats with blisters, and insects that would turn our veins to fire, and tornados and floods and thunderstorms.

He told us that most people didn't know anything about the world around them, what was really happening. But we would. He said the soft world was one where people made up reasons to worry and be scared. Where they created predators so they could pretend that they didn't live among actual ones. Where people thought they were safe just because they could turn on a light or hold a computer in their hand. But we were different. We were strong. We were aware. We would stand tall and alone and hard, and we would be the ones who knew how to *live*.

I know that speech, I remember those lessons, because he repeated them over and over. But standing here, I remember more, too. I remember those hours on the first day when it was just me and Mom. Alex told us to find a stream, that we'd make our camp nearby. And so, while he went to talk to bankers and virtual survivors, we went into the woods.

Finding the water took a long time. Mom marked our path

with red yarn so we could find our way back to the clearing with the tent, and the skein was getting smaller and smaller.

But finally we saw it. A creek. We didn't yet know about leeches and smaller parasites that can torment your insides, so when we spotted the clear water, we immediately turned our hands into cups and let it pour down our throats. The rocks under our feet were smooth, and we stood in the middle of the water, letting it tickle and hug our legs. We threw handfuls toward the sun, so the water glistened like fireworks. I don't know who laughed first, me or Mom. But soon we both were dancing right in that water, throwing it so high that it felt like rain. So high that Mom could pretend like she wasn't crying. That she wasn't breaking the rule and thinking about *him*, remembering him, how he would never dance like this, dipping his knees and throwing his chubby arms into the air. How *that* morning, the day that changed everything, she had danced down the hall, happy that he had slept through the night for the first time, how Dad had twirled her in a circle as she pranced by him, how she had been singing about him being her sunshine, her only sunshine, when she opened the door to see that he hadn't been sleeping at all. I wish that moment before were a loop, her dancing in the hall, never opening that door, that moment when we didn't know how everything could be wrong and right all at once.

Don't call us Mom and Dad anymore.

"Who is Matthew?"

I blink and shake my head. The edges of my vision blur. I didn't lose that much blood, but the crash might've affected my ears. There's a tunnel inside ears. Pressure has to be equal on the inside and outside of that tunnel, or people feel dizzy. The free fall and impact of the landing could've affected that pressure. Adrenaline pulsing through my veins could do it too.

"Who is Matthew?" Hayes repeats.

"My brother," I say, then shake my head again.

"I didn't know you—"

"I don't. We need to take stock of what we have. Supplies. That's number one. Anything we can use to get through the night."

"Someone will find us before nightfall," Hayes says.

I huff. "No one knows where we are, Hayes. We messed up." Something about saying it out loud makes my heart settle, my breathing get normal again. Maybe that's part of what "taking stock" means; facing up to what you have and what you've done. I nod to myself. I messed up, but now I'm going to fix it.

"But your grandma . . ." Hayes hasn't taken stock of anything yet. He stands in front of me, a bruise blooming on his cheek, helmet still on, bloody mouth opening and closing like a goldfish's. "Nanny Pat will see that your plane is missing and figure it out! Everyone knows that you'd be going to Pando, that it's where you wanted your first flight to be. She'll tell Chief Skip, they'll head in this direction, and they'll find us!"

"*You* knew," I correct him. "*You* knew that my first flight would be to Pando. No one else ever heard me. And Nanny Pat is going to CAP headquarters, down in Cedar City. She won't be back until tomorrow." I squeeze Hayes's shoulder with my good hand. "Our parents are going to think we ran off. They're going to be looking at your house and then mine. Then the woods, maybe? Probably the school or any other dumb place regular kids would run. We're about thirty miles outside of where they'd think to look." I glance around. "We're in the middle of the Canyon Mountains." I didn't want to be caught, so I flew over the ridges without roads or houses. "No one's coming for us. We've got to get out on our own."

He goldfishes some more.

"Face it, Hayes. We're spending the night." I ease Nanny Pat's emergency kit off my back and finally look down at my arm. The white metal of the hinge is buried into the skin except for a half-inch triangle, which means about a full inch of metal is embedded. The edge of the hinge hits the deep scratch I got this morning from the rusty gas can. The skin around both injuries is puffy and red, but the blood isn't gushing from it anymore. It's more like the glugs from the tipped-over gas can. I don't think it nicked a vein.

The world gets fuzzy around the sides of my vision again. *Focus, Gerty. Take stock.*

I breathe out. "Listen, Hayes. Here's what's going to happen. You're going to reach into the cockpit and pull out your mom's Pulaski."

"Wait, what?" Hayes asks. "I can reach in there? Are you sure it's not going to blow up?"

I sigh. "No. It's not going to blow up. Listen. Next, you're going to use the edge of the ax part and *carefully* cut at the canvas strips of fabric that create the seat. You're going to make sure you get the biggest pieces you can. You're going to run the edge of the blade along the line of screws on the wing skin. It's like polyester—it'll be stiff, too, but better than nothing. Got it?"

Hayes nods. I'm moving slower than I ought to be, and my breath is too loud in my head. I unzip the pack and pull out the first aid kit. Opening it, I look for antiseptic spray. It's missing. . . . I never put it back after Hayes hurt his finger. I do have long gauze bandages, which I lay on the ground with my good hand. There's a needle and thread, a bottle of iodine, and some matches in there too. An empty flask rattles in the bottom.

"You'll keep as much of the fabric together as you can," I tell him. My knees wobble a little as another glob of blood hits my boot. "Go on, get the Pulaski. That's first. Then come here."

Hayes pauses a second, then lunges toward the plane. His fingers tangle in the bungee cord. Adrenaline. It's pumping too much in both of us. Forgivable. He turns back to me, a smile tugging on his face when he frees the Pulaski, I guess realizing he isn't going to blow up after all. I don't roll my eyes. They're not working so great right now. "What are you going to do?" he asks. "While I cut up the seat, I mean."

I nod toward the kit supplies. "I'm getting to that."

Hayes nods. His color is coming back. Having a focus point can pull a person back from panic. That's why Alex says to keep a list going, no matter what. Huge problems are solved step by step. *How do you eat an elephant, Gerty? Bite by bite. That's why we make a list. Focus small.* I lick my lips. "Okay, great. You need to do one thing before that. I'm going to yank this metal out of my arm. Then you're going to squeeze the gash together and wrap my arm with gauze. *Tight.*"

Hayes trembles but his eyes stay focused. That's good. "Then what?"

Black spots burst in front of me as I grab that little metal triangle. "Then I'm going to pass out."

15

CHIEF SKIP

Chief Skip is sitting behind a desk in the middle of the station, but his mind is on the wildfire. How safe is Rabbit? If the trajectory stays the same, the town should be clear from damage, but he mentally catalogs all the outliers in town, who wouldn't be connected enough to hear potential evacuation orders. Already his mom's been hounding him to track down his wayward brother and make sure he stays out of trouble. But when has Skip ever been able to keep his brother in line?

All around him is chaos and noise—phones ringing, uniformed officers rushing in and out, televisions on in corners, radios blaring. It smells like sweat, coffee, and bleach all at once. But as a man enters the office, Skip's eyes immediately dart to the newcomer.

Almost as though conjured by his thoughts, there's his brother. Sparky's sporting a patchy mustache these days, likely trying to make his baby face seem older. Though relief pumps through him—now he can tell Ma that he saw Sparky and that he's doing fine—Skip doesn't smile.

"It's a busy day, Sparky," he says. He's tired, practically able to see the shadowed swollen circles under his own eyes. He runs a hand through his dark hair, stopping when he sees the same action mirrored in his brother. He pushes away a thought about whether such traits are genetic and somehow that's the only one they share, that he got everything decent his folks had to offer while Sparky got the worst bits. *Stop it,* he tells himself. *You don't know that he's up to anything bad* this *time.*

"I know you're busy," Sparky says, his voice squeaky. He pushes his hands into his pant pockets. He seems hesitant, and his mouth twitches. He's probably expecting Skip to mention the contractor job he'd set up for Sparky, only for him to be a no-show. But what's the point of even asking Sparky why he blew it off? It's not like he'd hear the truth.

Skip clenches his jaw, wondering when Sparky will go too far, and knowing he'll be the one to snap the handcuffs around his brother's skinny wrists. "What do you want, Sparky?"

"The fire. I wondered what you could tell me about it. Is . . . is Ma going to be okay? The house?"

Skip raises an eyebrow. He doesn't speak for a heavy minute. Sparky glances toward the door. Finally Skip shakes his head. Years of training on how to read people, and his kid brother still manages to surprise him. "We're evacuating down toward

Bryce Canyon, but nothing here yet. If the wind shifts, who knows, but for now it seems to be moving slow, toward the west. I talked to Ma an hour ago. She's getting a bag ready, just in case."

Sparky nods. "That's, uh, good."

"Chief!" the receptionist calls. "We've got a situation. Woman named Tara's here. She says—"

"Bring her in!" Skip says, and jumps to his feet. Sparky steps back as Tara rushes into the room. Her eyes are wide, scanning the station, her face pale.

"Tara," Skip says softly. Worry lines her face; he crosses his arms to keep from reaching toward her. "All good?"

"Hayes," she says. "He ran off this morning and isn't back yet. He's not answering his phone. I tried the tracking app, and it's not showing him anywhere." Another officer comes in to drop a file on Skip's desk. He notices how Tara's body stills until the officer retreats.

Skip's eyes drag from Tara's clenched jaw to her eyes. "When's the last time you saw him?"

"This morning. About ten thirty or so. We . . . we had a fight," she says. "He was upset."

Skip opens a bottle of water and hands it to her. He glances at the clock on the wall when she takes a sip. It's a little after five o'clock. Hayes could still be burning off steam from the fight.

"Can I have one of those waters?" Sparky asks. Skip ignores him.

Tara pulls a picture from her back pocket. "Hayes's school picture. I don't know; I thought maybe you'd want . . ."

"I don't think we're to the point where we need to get his photo out," Skip says, but he grabs the picture. "I'll hang on to it, just in case."

Sparky leans forward. He snaps his fingers and points to the photo of Hayes. "Hey, I know this kid! I saw him the other day. He was stealing a grocery cart from behind the Quik Mart. Doofus took an empty, broken one. I told him if you're going to nab something, at least make it worth your while. Am I right?"

Skip blinks at him. Tara's mouth pops open. "Hayes wouldn't steal," she finally says.

Sparky cocks an eyebrow at her in a silent, *Sure, lady.*

Skip leans forward over the desk, trying to block out his brother. "Have you checked with his friends?"

"He doesn't have any," Tara says. Sparky laughs, and both Skip and Tara turn and stare at him. He puts up his hands and mouths, "Sorry."

"Sure he does," Skip says. "I see him with Gerty. Tough kid. Lives off the grid, survivalist family." If he's with her or her family, he'll be out of cell phone range, and that could explain why he hasn't responded to Tara's texts or calls. A siren blares as a fire truck barrels past the station, heading south. "Gerty's a great kid," he says, trying to reassure Tara. "But don't get her started on forest fires. She thinks she's an expert on pretty much everything. She most likely is, too."

Tara rubs her temple with her thumb. "Figures you'd know more than me about my son." Skip swallows. He's always saying the wrong thing with her. The radio blares, announcing that a spike fire camp will be setting up in Beaver. "I really thought things would be different on the outs."

On the outs. Skip sees his brother tilt his head at the inmate phrase for life outside the prison. He clears his throat and shakes his head at Sparky, curtailing him from asking about Tara's incarceration.

Suddenly Tara's eyes widen. "My Pulaski," she gasps.

Skip holds his hand up like a stop sign. "I think they've got plenty of help for the wildfire right now, Tara. Let's focus on Hayes."

She shakes her head. "My Pulaski was missing this morning. I thought he hid it because we—Jacey and I—were talking about going to the camp. Skip, what if . . . what if Hayes took it? What if he and this Gerty kid are going *toward* the fire?"

Skip fights the urge to grin at her using his first name and focuses on her words. "You're taking some big leaps there." He pulls on his jacket and his hat. It's a bit soon to consider Hayes missing, but what does it hurt to look around? And if it means that the next time Tara says his name, she does so with a smile, well, that won't hurt either. "I'll patrol. Make some calls from the road. We'll find him."

"Can I come with you?" Her voice is small.

Skip strides around the desk. He catches himself reaching out to take her elbow, and he smooths his hand on his leg instead when she crosses her arms. "Let's head toward the fire camp, see if anyone's spotted the kids."

"What about me?" Sparky calls as they rush past.

"I'll tell Ma you asked about her, Sparky," he says without looking back.

When they get to the patrol car, Skip spots his brother sliding into the passenger seat of a blue sedan. He recognizes the driver as another troublemaker, nicknamed Whistle. There's a third man in the back seat. Skip would bet his pension it's Lonnie, who most recently was on his radar for poisoning a neighbor's dog. He sighs, any hope of Sparky turning a new leaf crumbling as Whistle throws his arm around his brother's shoulder.

"Is something wrong?" Tara asks, standing beside the door without getting in. "Is it okay for me to ride with you? I can follow if you'd rather I not be in the passenger seat—"

Skip tears his eyes from his brother and turns them back to Tara. He notes the fear in her expression, knowing it's separate from the panic she's feeling over Hayes. Going to the police station, asking for help, it took tremendous bravery for someone used to seeing cops from the other side of bars. "No, please," he says. "I could use your help."

"I don't know how much help I can be," she says, but does

open the door to sit beside him. "Hayes barely talks to me."

"It'll get better," he says. "All kids can be jerks sometimes when they're his age."

"I deserve it more than most moms," she mutters.

"That's not true," he says firmly. "You're here. You love him. That's enough. Now let's find him."

16

HAYES

Gerty's been out for a long time. Or maybe it's only been fifteen minutes. I don't know, except the sun is barely hanging in the sky now and has turned a deep orange color. It's so quiet.

Gerty gave me work to do, but all I want to do is watch to make sure she's breathing. My mouth feels packed with cotton and fumes, even though nothing actually exploded like I thought it would. After she pulled the metal from her arm, Gerty breathed out twice and then closed her eyes, slumping against me. For a minute I thought she'd died, even though she had told me she was going to pass out. One good thing about being stranded on the side of a mountain in the middle of nowhere? No one saw me act a fool, sobbing like a baby while I wrapped her arm and watched her breaths.

I used the Pulaski to cut the fabric from the plane seat

like she told me to, but every minute I came back and made sure she was still breathing. When the sun started to bake her face, I grabbed her under her arms and dragged her so she was shaded by the wreckage.

Now all the thoughts I don't want to have slam around my skull. The conveyer belt Mrs. Freid talked about—the one that filters people's thoughts—must've malfunctioned in the crash, because the thoughts are whipping out so fast, none are fully formed. Has Mom noticed I'm gone yet? Is she looking for me? Would anyone think to come here? Where *is* here? Are there bears around? Cougars? How long does it take to die from thirst? Will we freeze tonight? Will Gerty ever wake up? Will she be the same? Will she know what to do? Is Charlie still mad at me? Will Gerty ever see Pando now? Can you starve in one day? What if the fire heads toward us? What if Mom doesn't even notice I'm—

"Hey." I startle and there is Gerty, twisting her arm to inspect her bandage. "Not bad." She squints at me as she unties her sweatshirt from around her waist with her good arm. "You look awful."

And it's like she's shoved all those thoughts into a garbage can. Because there she is, her face pale and dirty, her arm cradled against her side, her wrecked plane behind her, telling *me* I look awful. "Well, I was in a plane crash," I say, my voice thick from all the screaming I did while she was out. She pushes herself up so we're sitting side by side.

"No kidding," Gerty says as she slips her good arm into her sweatshirt and shrugs it over to drape across her hurt side. "Hope the pilot's okay." I snort and then we're laughing. Not just a chuckle, either, both of us cackling so hard that we're leaning into each other.

We're nestled in a crevice in the side of the mountain, the sun sinking behind it. And despite everything, I've never seen anything more beautiful than this sunset or heard anything better than Gerty's laughter.

We gather rocks and build a ring, clearing the thistle sage from inside it with our shirts covering our skin. I made the mistake of grabbing one with my bare hand, and it still stings. "We need to find water," Gerty says as we pile sticks in the ring. She strikes a match and lights some of the sage before tucking it under the kindling.

I try not to notice how swollen my tongue feels.

Gerty nudges me. "Roll your tongue around your mouth. Ten times in one direction, ten in the other. It'll get your spit going."

It works, but not nearly enough. Gerty nods when I swallow a moment later. "Good thing you stay calm, Hayes. I didn't think you had it in you, but you proved me wrong! Just think how much worse you'd feel if you had wasted all your moisture crying and screaming when we crashed."

I decide not to mention what exactly happened while she was passed out.

The stench from the fire tickles my nose, but when the flame goes red around the larger twigs, the smoke isn't as thick.

"That's what we need to do first thing tomorrow. Find water," Gerty says. "When we find a stream, we'll follow it toward the river. Then we'll be closer to where we can find people."

People. My heart trills as hard as it did when we were falling. The things I said to Mom come back to me. Those words stripped away the hard expression she'd worn since getting out. I didn't like what I saw underneath it, didn't like facing how much I'd hurt her. *She* was the one who had ripped my life to shreds as easily as she had scraped the popcorn ceiling back in California. *She* was the one who'd hurt me. "What about Pando?" I blurt.

Gerty blinks at me. "What about him?"

"Don't you still want to see him?" Around us, stars bloom in the darkening sky. Mom will have noticed by now that I'm not home. Grandma Louise will have called Chief Skip. "We're close, aren't we? Wouldn't it be just as easy to move toward Pando as it would anywhere else? I mean, I bet we're closer to Fishlake than we are to Rabbit."

"Water. Water is our first priority. But I think you're right—it makes more sense to go north toward Fishlake. We'll likely find a park ranger or something." Gerty leans forward and breathes into the flames, making them flare.

I let out my breath, and she pauses. "Why'd you get into the plane?" she whispers.

"What?"

"Why'd you get into the plane?" Gerty sits back. Her good arm is against me, the stiff fabric ripped from the plane wrapped around us both. Somewhere nearby something howls. I shift closer to her. "You know why I left," she continues, "but why did you?"

"Are you trying to say I caused the accident? Because I didn't do anything. I don't even think I moved much at all."

Gerty sighs. "No, *I* crashed. I startled when the bird flew in, then the engine stalled and I didn't correct like I should've. We were too close to the ground. That's on me. I'm asking why *you* got in the plane at all."

I don't say anything for a long time. Whatever was howling earlier yips now. Or I guess it could be a different something. "Maybe we should make the fire bigger," I say, and throw on more wood—one of the wing ribs Gerty worked so hard to build.

Gerty's hand circles my arm. "Hayes."

"My mom, okay?" I croak. "My mom wants to go to the fire camp. She wants to go back to being a firefighter." The rib collapses in the fire with a snap. "She already left us once. Now she wants to do it again."

Gerty doesn't say anything for a long time. "Matthew was my baby brother."

"I'm sorry," I whisper, because I know that's what you're supposed to say when someone dies.

Gerty sighs and leans against me. "I'm sorry too. About the crash. But I'm glad you're here. Even if you don't know what you're doing and will probably get us in worse trouble."

"Thanks," I scoff.

Two eyes shine in the darkness. I gasp. Gerty stares into the flames. "It's a fox. It's been hanging around for a while. I'm surprised it's this high up in the canyon. The coyotes probably flushed it out of the woods."

I try to swallow, but my mouth is so dry. "Is it going to attack us?"

Gerty shakes her head. "No. I'm not as sure about the coyotes. We've got to keep the fire going. We'll take turns being on watch, okay?"

Another howl rings out in the distance and the shining eyes disappear.

"I'll take first watch," I say. Gerty nestles closer and closes her eyes. I wrap my hand around the Pulaski handle and wait for the fox to appear again.

17

CHIEF SKIP

Chief Skip rubs the back of his neck. Across from where he's standing behind his desk sit Nanny Pat and Jennifer, who has the baby strapped to her chest. Tears stream silently down Jennifer's face, and her hands shake as she shifts Lilith to her other side. Standing behind them, still as a frightened rabbit, is Tara. His heart lurches at the sight of her, wondering how much terror it takes to freeze a mother in place like that. He clears his throat. "Let me get this straight. Gerty has been secretly building an airplane?"

Nanny Pat stiffens her spine. "I'd hardly call it secret. We've been working on it for months."

Jennifer snorts. "Paid for by money Gerty helped herself to from our reserves *without* our knowledge!"

Skip holds up his hands, stopping the cyclical argument he's already heard the two of them hash out twice since they rushed into the station before the sun this morning. "And you noticed the plane missing this morning," he directs to Nanny Pat.

She nods. "Affirmative. I returned late from Cedar City last night. It was too dark for me to notice whether the plane was in the barn. However, I would've heard her take off this morning, so I believe she must've left yesterday. As early as two o'clock, though likely later if she had the sense to do a precheck of the plane. That's when I left for Cedar City. She would know better than to take anything more than a one-hour first flight and wouldn't have gone at dark."

Jennifer whimpers. "How could she do this?"

Nanny Pat's chin lifts. "I don't know. I was supervising and laid clear conditions."

Jennifer hiccups and Nanny Pat's lip trembles at the sound.

Chief Skip looks away from them to stare down at his notes, trying to block the emotion pouring from the people in front of him so he can focus. "Sounds like those conditions got a little muddy. Seems clear to me now that both kids had reason to run. Between the fights they got into with y'all, the fact that they took the gear bag and the Pulaski, and what the school is telling me about fights and odd behavior, I don't think this is an abduction situation. Seems unlikely more than the two of them could've fit into the plane." Jennifer sobs, and the sound sets off the baby. "We've got crews looking for them, but what we really need is some direction. Where could they have gone?"

"I told you," Tara says, her voice hoarse. Chief Skip tries not to wince at the circles under her eyes. "Hayes took the Pulaski. He's going to the fire."

Chief Skip nods. "That's a possibility, for sure." He ignores the fury on Tara's face at the dismissal. "And the fire camp is on alert for the kids. But they've been looking skyward non-stop, judging the wind, and no one saw an ultralight. Where else could they've gone?"

The baby wails, and Jennifer's fingers can't seem to untie the knot in the carrier to remove her. Earlier, Chief Skip asked about Alex, and Jennifer simply shook her head.

Nanny Pat stands. Jennifer slumps, still hiccupping, as her mother kneels in front of her. "I'm sorry," she says. Hesitantly, her fingers shaking, she grasps Jennifer's shoulders. "I'm so sorry, honey." Jennifer droops forward, her head cradled in Nanny Pat's neck, the baby between them calming down.

The receptionist opens the door to the inner part of the station. "Skip, your brother is here."

Skip sighs, again rubbing the back of his neck. He glances up to see Sparky strolling into the office, grinning as he takes in Tara and then the others. "Kid still missing, eh?"

"Now's not a good time, Spark."

Thankfully, the women ignore the newcomer. Sparky leans against the wall, watching the rest of them like this is a movie.

"We have to find them," Tara says. "They've already been alone in the woods overnight. Who knows if they're hurt, if they know where they're going, if they're even—"

Jennifer pushes back from Nanny Pat's embrace. Her voice firm, she says, "They're alive. Gerty will get them out of any situation. They're fine."

Skip gives her a grim smile. "We'll increase the radius of where we've been searching now that we know they've been airborne and likely crashed."

"Those kids crashed? Like a plane?" Sparky says.

"Sparky, this is a really bad time," Skip growls. Figures his brother would take an interest in what he does when there are more crises unfolding than typically happen all year in Rabbit.

The receptionist throws open the door again. "Skip," she calls. "Bad news." All the parents rise to their feet, and she puts up her hands. "Sorry, poor choice of words. I mean regarding the fire. Winds shifted. The blaze is heading northwest now too. They're establishing an evacuation zone bordering that part of Fishlake."

Skip nods. "Put the deputies on it. The kids are my focus today." He turns to another officer, sitting at the desk behind him. "Put out word to the media. Get them the pictures of the kids. Ask for search party volunteers."

"Going to be hard with so many people getting ready to evacuate—" the officer says. His words cut off at Skip's expression. "Yes, sir. I'm on it."

"Thank you," Tara whispers.

"Whoa," Sparky says, as though to himself. "*Two* missing

kids. Crashed an airplane. *And* the fire's moving northwest. Plus, now places close to Fishlake are starting to evacuate? That's a lot, brother."

Skip blinks at Sparky, who salutes and backs out of the office. Skip tries not to sigh in relief that he's leaving, even as he spots Whistle's blue car in the lot. Whatever Sparky is up to is going to have to wait.

18

GERTY

Cold. That's my first thought. And then, *Fire.* My arm is on *fire.* I cry out and Hayes jumps to his feet. "What? What?" His face is red, and I realize he's ashamed at falling asleep during his watch.

But I never had a watch. He never woke me. I *never* sleep through the night without waking. How could I now, on the side of a mountain? I shift, and the slight jostle of my arm is enough to shake away any sleepiness. I pull off the sweatshirt draped around me. Still sprawled on the ground in front of the smoking embers, I gingerly touch the bandage, which is now crusty with dark brown discharge. The skin around the bandage is puffy and so red that it's nearly purple. Infection takes days to set in. This doesn't make sense. *You're fine,* I tell myself.

His eyes bugging, Hayes doesn't speak as I lift my arm, but he steps backward when I whimper. The skin under my arm is blackish blue. I can't lift my arm even to shoulder height. "I think it's broken," I say, and clear my throat to steady my voice. "I thought it was just the hinge that injured me, right on top of where I hurt my arm yesterday morning. But I think the bone fractured on impact too."

Hayes turns his forearm so I can see the bruise across the top. It's the same width as my arm. "I think your arm broke against mine when we landed," he says.

For a moment neither of us speaks. Finally I push myself up with my good arm. *Focus. Take stock.* "Well, it's a good thing I have two of them, then, huh?"

"We've got to get you to a doctor," Hayes says.

"I'm fine," I say, even though the ground is a little wobbly. *Focus.* People break bones all the time. I glance at our supplies, forming a plan. "I don't think the bone's displaced. Doctors wouldn't do anything I can't do. When Jennifer fell stepping out of the tub a couple months ago, she didn't go to the hospital. Alex wrapped her arm, and she held Lilith on the other side for a few weeks." I take a strip of the fabric we've cocooned ourselves in overnight. "Help me?"

Hayes nods and follows my instructions until my arm is cradled in a sling just like Alex fashioned for Jennifer. It'll be fine.

Hayes kicks dirt over the smoldering embers. He's rolling his tongue in his mouth, trying to use the trick I showed him last night to be less thirsty. It won't work. I'm sure his mouth feels as packed with grime as mine. We need water.

The fox we spotted the night before peeks out from behind a sage bush. I turn to point it out to Hayes, but he's already watching the animal. We bundle our supplies inside the fabric, and Hayes ties it into a pack slung across his back. His hands shake as he makes the knot. I want to tell him it's going to be okay, that by now Nanny Pat has to have noticed the missing plane. But why would anyone look for us *here*? Besides, I don't know if his hands are shaking because he's scared or because he's hungry and thirsty.

"Let's go," Hayes says, and it feels like he's stealing my words.

Getting down the ravine is slippery business. The range folds in on itself, with huge outcrops of shale like the spikes of a dinosaur popping out often enough to be inconvenient. The sky is gray and foggy. I wish it would rain, and the thought makes me shudder as I imagine the water on my skin and in my mouth.

One time Alex and I didn't have luck catching trout during a hike. We had to go all the way back without anything to eat. The whole hike, we pretended we were eating a feast. "The thing is, Gerty," he said then, "if I tell you not to think about an ostrich, what pops into your head?" Before I could answer, he nodded. "Ostrich. Nothing but ostrich. That's why it's better just to let yourself think of stuff. Otherwise, all your energy is spent trying not to think about it."

Kind of strange, then, that none of us talk about the crater in our chests, the one that split us nearly in half when Matthew died. I bite my lip to stop from crying out at the sudden, new flare of pain. I've thought of Matthew so much the past two days, more than I have in years. It feels like I'm betraying Alex and Jennifer. He was *theirs* more than he was mine, and they set the conditions on how we were going to remember—or not remember—him. But he was mine. He was mine, too.

"Does it hurt much?" Hayes asks, and I realize I must've made some sort of soft noise.

I shake my head. "No. I'm fine."

Finally we make it into some woods. The trees are clusters of narrow aspens, then merge into blue spruce, white fir, Douglas fir. I point out the varieties to Hayes as we walk.

"Are we heading in the right direction?" Hayes asks a couple of times.

"Yep," I tell him, squinting through the canopy to look at the position of the sun. "We're heading north, toward Pando."

"How long do you think we've been walking?"

"A couple hours." I nod toward a tree, and he ties a thread around the trunk. We've been marking the trees every six feet or so. I glance behind me, seeing faintly the red loops around trees in a somewhat straight line of trunks behind us. I wish I knew what time it was. It already looks close to sunset, which doesn't make any sense. We've been walking a long time, but no way it's been *that* long.

"And you think we'll find some water soon?" Hayes rubs at his throat.

Then he stops, throwing his arm out to stop me, too, as ahead of us the fox dashes across our path. The animal vanishes into the woods in an instant.

"What do you think that was about?" Hayes whispers. "I hope whatever it was running from doesn't head this way."

We both jump when a branch snaps in the woods. Then a fat squirrel scampers up the tree near us, and Hayes lets out a shaky sigh. We smile at each other, and it feels so much like crying.

"Look!" I gasp, pointing to where the fox headed. "His footprint! The ground is muddy. That means . . ." But I don't need to finish. *Water!* Hayes strides ahead, and there it is, a narrow trickle of water. He sinks his hand into it, but I slap away his fingers before he can lick them. "We need to treat any water. Let's follow it, see if we can find the source."

Hayes growls but follows me. The trickle turns into a narrow stream, about the width of my arm, as we head up an incline. I know that to get back to a town ranger station, we should be heading down the mountain, not back up the other side, but I can hear the water now. We're like those cartoon animals that smell a pie baking, the scent alone making them float toward the source. We're pushing through trees, not feeling the scratches from the limbs on our cheeks or the tumble down to our knees over roots as we scramble toward that delicious sound. *Water!*

And then it's there, sliding down the shale in lazy gushes. I want to unhinge my jaw and make my throat a bucket for it to pour into. Hayes is turning his hands into cups to capture it, laughing as it runs through his fingers. "We have to treat it," I remind him and myself, even as the cotton feeling in my mouth threatens to suffocate me. I pull out the flask from the emergency kit.

"Hurry," Hayes says.

I put the edge of my T-shirt over the opening of the flask and hold it under the stream. My shirt's dirty but still a better filter than nothing, considering all the algae and leaf bits that are flowing down the stream. It must be from melted snow at the mountaintop; while it's a steady trickle, the water isn't rushing. When the flask is filled, I pull the stopper from the dark iodine bottle and add three drops. Too much iodine is toxic. Not enough, and whatever is living in the water could also kill us, or at least make us super sick.

"Is that it?" Hayes asks. Inside I'm shrugging—I have no idea if it's the right amount of iodine—but I nod anyway as I pinch the flask between my knees and screw on the lid with my good hand. "Okay," he says. "Who goes first?"

"We have to wait," I tell him.

"How long?"

I wince. "About a half hour." I sink into the soft dirt beside the stream. "We're going to be here awhile."

Hayes presses a fist into his stomach. Now that the water is *right here*, everything else that is wrong seems to fall in line, waiting to be addressed. How we're going to get home, whatever is wrong with my arm, how much trouble we're in, and—mostly—how hungry we are.

"Let's get some food," I say, and grab some of the reedy grass beside the stream. "Do what I do," I tell him. Hayes kneels beside me, grass in his hand. I crumble it in my fingers and rub it on my forearm, ignoring the flare of pain above my elbow at the motion. "Now we wait. If we don't have any hives or anything in ten minutes, then we can chew some and spit it out."

"Oh, joy," Hayes mutters. He copies my movements with a sigh and then leans back on his haunches.

I ignore him. "And then if it doesn't fill our mouths with hives after another fifteen minutes, we can eat some."

"And we won't get sick?"

"Not necessarily, but we shouldn't die. It's called a sensitivity test."

Hayes groans but rubs more grass into his arm. His groan turns into a yelp, and he jumps to his feet. He shakes his hand, throwing off a few dozen black ants. The grass he yanked must've been right over a hill of them. He says a bad word and scowls at me when I cheer.

"Settle down!" I say. "This is an awesome discovery." I pinch one of the ants and pop it into my mouth, crunching down. "A snack we don't have to wait to eat!"

"You're disgusting," Hayes says after blinking at me for a solid three seconds, enough time for me to nab four more ants.

"Mmm!" I say with a grin.

19

HAYES

Here's something I never wanted to know: ants taste like lemonade mix.

In fact, Gerty throws a few into the flask. She says it'll counteract the iodine taste a little. "And add interesting texture." I wonder if, when we crashed, she got knocked in the head despite the helmet.

Munching on handfuls of ants doesn't fill a belly, but it's better than not eating anything. My mouth goes from feeling like it's stuffed with an old sock to feeling like I sucked on citrus coffee grounds. The grass hasn't made either of our arms or mouths itchy, but it takes a long time to chew into something we can swallow. It's a little more filling than the ants.

Finally Gerty says it's safe to drink the water. I gulp three huge swallows. It's cold and wet, and that more than makes up for the metal-tinged mud flavor. Gerty grabs the flask from me and downs some of her own. Then she refills the flask and adds the drops.

"Should we wait here?" I ask. The sun never really came out today, but it looks like soon it will be evening. I hate the idea of spending another night outside. An owl hoots in the distance, but it's eerily quiet. *Too* quiet for woods, I think.

Gerty chews her lip. "We probably should wait another half hour. Then we can drink this," she says, raising the flask, "and refill it."

I nod, already thirsty again, but my stomach doesn't feel quite as empty thanks to the ants. If only they had been bigger; I wouldn't have had to eat so many. "Look!" I cheer as a cricket hops between us.

"Stop!" Gerty calls as I swipe it up and pop it into my mouth. Whatever, she can find her own bug. She grimaces as I crunch down. And then I try not to throw up all my ants and grass.

Here's something else I never wanted to know: crickets taste like pee and dirt. Even worse? They're crunchy on the outside and gooey—*very* gooey—on the inside.

"I tried to warn you," Gerty says as she sinks beside me.

A half hour is a long time to wait when your mouth is filled with cricket goo.

"Do you know where we're going?" I ask a few hours later. I've been really tired before—after running a mile in gym class and then playing football at recess. And I've been scared—that first night in the group home, wondering if Mom was okay; all those times she was in fires and no one told us if she'd made it out okay. But those memories feel about as painful as a paper cut compared with the ripped-apart tired and scared I am now. My legs barely hold me. I don't know why I'm shaking, only that I can't stop.

Gerty nods, but I see her squinting upward a lot. It's so cloudy and the trees so dense, we can't make out where the sun is in the sky. "We're heading north. I'm sure of it," she says.

But then I spy a red thread tied around a tree. One of *our* trees. "Gerty." She stills and something flashes across her face. It's panic, I think. A memory I don't want slams me. My mom's face looked a lot like Gerty's just did when the judge sentenced her. Like Gerty, her eyes darted to mine as though measuring whether I understood what had happened. I didn't then. I do now. We've circled, somehow, and are right back to where we were this morning.

I want to scream at Gerty, the fury rushing through me more foul than a chomped-up cricket. How can we be right where we started? She made me feel like she knew what she was doing. She was supposed to know what she was doing!

Gerty's bottom lip trembles. "I thought I knew . . . I'm doing what I'm supposed to."

I swallow my anger. "Well, that didn't work out. Let's go this way." I point toward the left. Maybe it's west? I don't know.

Gerty cradles her hurt arm close to her body. She licks her dry lips. "I can make a compass. I bet there's a magnet on the plane somewhere. . . ." She lowers the emergency pack and unzips it, muttering something about a cork.

"We don't have any of those things," I whisper. I yank another thread from the fabric and tie it around a new tree in the opposite direction from where we've been going. "Let's go."

We don't talk for a long time. The sky turned orangish red and now is darkening. The air feels heavy, too thick to fill my lungs. Earlier Gerty said that it was the wildfire smoke, but not to worry. Even if the flames were still in Bryce Canyon, the smoke could travel hundreds of miles.

"I'm sorry," she says as we walk through the dark. "I'm supposed to know stuff, how to get out of this. I thought I knew—"

"You know a lot," I tell her. I catch myself as I trip on a root.

"But I'm the one who crashed. I'm the one who got hurt, and I'm the one who led us in circles."

I use the Pulaski to lift a branch so Gerty can go under it. We've been heading downhill for a while, looking for another stream. The plan is to camp there for the night so we can fill up the flask again and again. My mouth is so dry. I shiver and shove my hands deep into my jean pockets. I wish I had worn boots like Gerty. My toes squish in my sneakers, still damp from stepping into the creek hours earlier. Something howls in the distance, and something else responds to it, closer. When a twig snaps a few yards away, I tell myself it's another fat squirrel or the fox that's been following us around. It's too dark to see anything.

Gerty is hunched as she passes me, her hurt arm so close to her body, even with the brace, that I know she must be hurting a lot. "You landed the plane." She stills for a moment, so I know she hears me. "We got out of it because of you. You kept going, even though you're hurt. You made sure we had good water to drink and food that didn't make us sick. You know a lot."

"But I don't know how to get us out of here."

"We'll figure it out," I tell her, letting the branch drop behind me just as something in the woods screeches. I jump ahead, right into Gerty, who has turned into a statue in front of me. "Gerty?"

My feet slide on gravel. *Gravel?*

That's when I realize we've entered a clearing. The smoky clouds part enough for moonlight to fall on a little wood cabin with a chicken coop beside it.

"We're safe!" I yelp.

But Gerty's hand wraps around my wrist. "Why are all the lights off?"

"It's late. Maybe everyone's in bed."

Gerty shakes her head. "No, something's wrong." She points. "The door is wide open on the chicken coop."

"Maybe it's a summer cabin," I say. "Or, like, only used for fishing or hunting?"

"There's a full trash can," she says, pointing to the canisters beside the garage with her chin.

I shrug. "So what? It has a roof and walls. Probably running water, too." Another howl pierces behind us in the woods. Too close. "Gerty, we've got to get inside."

Gerty doesn't say anything.

"C'mon," I tell her. "Maybe they left a door unlocked or a key under the mat if they're not home. Maybe they have a landline or a computer or something, and we can let our families know we're okay."

Gerty steps backward. "What if it isn't safe?"

"Of course it's safe!" I tell her. "Safe as houses."

20

GERTY

My arm is its own wildfire.

I know I should check it, but every time I move, I want to throw up.

The back door slides open into a kitchen with gleaming yellow wood floors, white cabinets and countertops, and a basket of eggs in the middle of a wooden table. Dirty dishes are piled in the sink, crumbs are scattered around the toaster, and there's an inch of cold coffee in the pot. "Hello?" Hayes calls, and then walks inside. "Hello!"

No one answers.

I go to the table and pick up one of the eggs. Is Alex planning to bring Donald and the rest of the flock along when we go to Oregon? Did they already leave? Are they waiting for me?

"I'm going to see if they have a house phone," Hayes says.

I trail behind him as he turns on lights and heads down the hall. There are clean rectangles along the hallway where artwork or photographs used to hang. Something thumps in my chest at the empty spots. Hayes doesn't hesitate, and I know he hasn't noticed them.

We pause in the doorway of the bedroom. A handmade quilt hangs like artwork on the wall. The bed is neatly made, but the dresser drawers are open, with a trail of clothes scattered across the floor. It's out of place in the orderly little house. There's a big black safe on the floor of the closet, the door shut.

"They left in a hurry," I say.

"Maybe they're just messy," Hayes says.

Across the hall from the bedroom is a small room with a desk. There's a dust-free square on the black desktop but no computer. There are a bunch of cords, though, as if someone grabbed the laptop but left those behind. A file cabinet is open, folders spilling out of it, and papers strewn on the floor.

A news flyer is on the floor next to the printer.

EVACUATION NOTICE: Sevier County, Utah, is under an immediate evacuation order due to threat of wildfire in the region. This is a Level III order. Take family, pets, and necessary items for at least a three-day period. Remember important papers and current medication. Consult the Sevier County Red Cross, informing them of where you and your family will be staying even if you do not intend to stay at the shelter. Drive with lights on, safely and slowly, out of the evacuation zone.

It's dated and time-stamped at one o'clock today. I glance at the clock hanging on the wall of the little office. It's nine o'clock at night.

The winds must've shifted.

"What do we do?" Hayes asks. I didn't realize he was reading the notice over my shoulder.

"What can we do?" I ask. A part of me knows I should be worried. A series of facts swim through my head. Like that wildfire can move more than six miles an hour in dense woods like those we're amid. That we're in a house made of wood planks on a remote, empty road. That no one knows where we are. And that it still might be the safest place we could be right now, compared with being alone in the forest.

Hayes's eyes unfocus. "The fire department will send out crews. They'll go door-to-door to make sure everyone is out," he says. "My mom did that. They'll do it too."

I nod, not bothering to tell him that might have already happened. That this family and the neighbors probably already contacted the Red Cross. I go into the bathroom and wash my face with one hand, using the creamy white soap beside the sink. It smells like Mrs. Freid, fresh and clean. For a wild moment I wonder if this is her house. I realize I haven't had to go to the bathroom for a long time, and I drink water from the spigot.

"No phone here, I guess. I'm going to check for other houses," Hayes says. He's holding a big black flashlight, flicking it on and off. "Maybe we just didn't see any in the dark. Maybe one of them has a landline or a radio or something."

I nod as I press a fluffy towel against my damp cheeks. I should go with him. But I want to keep pretending this little house is mine. My brain feels foggy, probably from hunger or from so much adrenaline. I know the house isn't safe, but it feels like nothing bad could ever happen here.

I drop the towel when I picture Jennifer dancing down the hallway. Bad things can happen anywhere, anytime.

But Hayes already left.

"Nothing," Hayes says a few minutes later, stepping back through the sliding door into the house. "I didn't see any houses around and I didn't want to go too far."

Hayes's stomach growls loudly, and I crack a smile. I hand him a plate of scrambled eggs. I made them with real butter I found in the fridge, but having used one hand means there are a few eggshells. Hayes doesn't seem to notice. "Isn't this, like, stealing?" he says as he plows a forkful into his mouth.

I laugh. "I can go try to find some ants if it makes you feel better about it."

He brings the plate in closer to his chest as he shovels more eggs onto his fork. "I peeked in the coop. There are some chickens sleeping inside. I guess they'll make more." He stills for a second, then scrapes some eggs onto a different plate. He shrugs at my eyebrow raise. "The fox is out there. Maybe this'll keep him from eating the chickens." He chews his lip as though reconsidering.

"I'll make more eggs," I tell him, and am answered with a grin. I scramble the rest of the eggs while he puts the plate outside in the yard. I tell Hayes we should rest only for an hour. Two at the most. Then we should head down the road toward, hopefully, town.

Soon we're sitting on the couch in the living room. We're drinking hot cocoa mixed with a can of evaporated milk that Hayes found in a cabinet. There are even little marshmallows on the top. It tastes like Christmas morning used to. He laughs when I run my finger through the dark sludge at the bottom of the mug and lick it. "Bleh!" It's salty, with none of the sweetness I expected. "That's so gross!"

"I should've stopped you, but it's payback for the cricket," Hayes says.

Hayes is dunking toast into his cocoa. I relax into the couch cushions and close my eyes.

"Gerty, we can't stay long. There has to be a town nearby."

I should be telling *him* what our next steps should be. I shouldn't be soft like this, sitting on a couch pretending it's

ours, that we could stay here forever. I could hunt and garden. Hayes could take care of the chickens. I don't realize I'm
daydreaming out loud until Hayes says he's a little scared of
chickens. I laugh and curl onto my side, pulling the blanket
that hangs over the couch with me.

My arm is a wildfire, but we're safe as houses.

I'm inside our house. No. I'm inside a cabin. Hayes is in front
of me, calling my name.

His face is an inch from mine, and it looks like he's screaming, but he isn't. He's whispering. "Gerty, wake up! Wake up
right now."

Fire! I feel it scorching my arm, all the way to my shoulder,
and want to scream, but his hand is over my mouth.

"Someone's here," he hisses.

21

HAYES

An orange light glows outside the windows, illuminating Gerty's face. It takes her way too long to wake up from whatever dream she's having. She gasps and I cover her mouth with my hand.

Someone flips on the light in the kitchen, right behind us. They step on the broken glass from the rock they threw through the sliding glass door. The door wasn't even locked. Whoever smashed it isn't the homeowner back for something they forgot, and I have a hunch that means they aren't going to let us borrow their phone to call our parents.

We slide down the side of the couch. If we can get to the hall, maybe we can hide under a bed until they leave.

"You know the drill," someone says. His voice is nasally, the end of each word blending into the next with a whistle. "Look for anything we can sell or pocket."

Someone else enters the house, their footsteps crunching the glass.

Gerty stills, then inches forward to peek over the edge of the couch. I fight the urge to yank her back by her ankles, but she scurries backward almost instantly. "We've got to get out of here," she whispers. "That's the same guy who was scoping out my house."

A third person walks in. "How long do we have, Whistle?"

The guy with the nasally voice says, "This house? Long as we want. Not another one around for miles. All the firefighters are clear on the other side of the mountain. With the other two Marystown houses I want to hit tonight, we've got to be quick. They're right next to each other." I hear a splash, and then a pungent, sharp odor hits my nose.

"Aw, come on, man," says one of them while the other laughs like a hyena. "Do we really have to do this?"

Whistle chuckles, ending in a high-pitched sound that would make a dog howl. "Quit braying like a donkey. It's freaking genius, Sparky! When they see the smoke, the fire-fighting crew and police will come here. Then we hit the Marystown houses back where they were. Keep 'em running in circles! Everyone blames the wildfire. No one's the wiser, our pockets are full."

"That's not the way it works," the other guy—Sparky—says. "I told you! Firefighters track the spread. They'll know this isn't the same fire."

Whistle laughs again. "Then we blame the missing kids. Police are out searching all over for them anyway, as if two twerps had any chance of surviving a plane crash, let alone being in the forest for two days."

"Yeah," pipes in the third guy. "The parents are convinced the kids are trying to fight the fire. Makes sense if they didn't find one, they'd light one." Something smashes. "It's what I would do."

"What?" Sparky mutters. "You were a messed-up kid, Lonnie."

"From the sounds of it, so are they," Lonnie says with a chuckle. "Did you say the one's mom was in jail? And the other's folks are loons living off the grid? People will believe those kids would do anything."

Sparky laughs. "Well, if they made it through a plane crash and a couple days in the woods, they probably *could* do anything they want."

Something crashes in the kitchen. Glass hits the floor. Sparky sighs. "Did you have to break the cabinet? The handle's right there."

My heart was already hammering fast, so I can't believe the jump it made when they started talking about me and Gerty. People are searching for us. They know about the plane crash! My body's pumping so much adrenaline that I can't be still, even though I know if these guys find us, they're not going to help us. No, these guys will *hurt* us.

Lonnie tells them he's going to scope out the garage. Gerty and I don't move, don't breathe, while he passes inches from the back of the couch and out the door in the kitchen that leads to the garage. He's close enough that I smell the cigarette smoke on him as he passes.

Gerty's hand squeezes mine. She points to the Pulaski on the floor between us and the couch, and then points to the hall.

Splash, splash, splash. I don't need to see it to know Whistle is drenching the gleaming kitchen with gasoline. I think about the quilt hanging on the wall, the basket on the table, the packets of cocoa in the cabinet.

"The fire is going to spread," the second guy says as Gerty crawls to a love seat across the room. She ducks behind it. I take a deep breath, grab the Pulaski, and follow her when he begins speaking again. "What if it gets out of control?"

"You worry too much, Sparky."

We make it to the bedroom. Gerty slowly, slowly closes the door. She holds the handle twisted to the side so it shuts with a soft click that nevertheless echoes in my head. Something crashes in the living room. One of the guys laughs. The china cabinet, maybe?

I open the window, wincing when the screen screeches as I cinch the tabs on the sides to pull it up. Part of me wants to crash through it, but I remember what Gerty's been saying over and over since we crashed. *Focus. Take stock.*

I gesture to her, and she climbs onto my bent leg to hoist

herself out the open window. I lower the Pulaski for Gerty to grab and then shove myself over the ledge. I land with a thud.

"What was that?" one of them shouts. It's the nervous one, Sparky.

Gerty and I press against the side of the house as flashlight beams sweep the yard from the living room window.

"Coyote, probably," Lonnie says. The flashlight sweeps again, catching shining eyes at the edge of the woods, too low to be a coyote. "Told you," he says. I silently thank the fox that's still trailing us.

The flashlight beam disappears as something else crashes inside the house. Gerty grabs my hand, and we dart across the yard to the chicken coop. I glance back over my shoulder and swear the nervous-sounding guy, Sparky, spots me. But he drops the curtain, so I must be mistaken.

We crouch inside, the birds cuddled together on a roost above us, seemingly barely noticing our presence. "What are we going to do?" I whisper.

Gerty doesn't answer. She is as still as a statue. Meanwhile, every cell in my body is telling me to run, run, run. But where?

A door opens and slams shut. "Bring the whole safe!" one of them yells to the other two. "We'll crack it back home."

I'm gripping the Pulaski so hard in my hands that my fingers cramp. Gerty presses a finger to my lips and shifts. She peeks out the little coop window. One of the birds shuffles, and there's a soft plop beside me, followed by a foul smell.

Seriously, chicken? Now? We're sort of in a crisis here! And for some reason that makes me want to laugh. A chuckle even tickles up my throat. But when I try to swallow it back, the sound that seeps from me is a sob. Gerty nabs a metal shovel with a long wooden handle hanging from a hook just inside the coop. She grasps it in her hand like a sword and kneels on the opposite side of the coop.

"What if someone's at home in the next house?" Sparky says as they hoist the safe toward the car.

"Why do you always worry so much, Spark?" Whistle grunts.

"No, seriously," he presses. "What would you do if someone spotted us? I mean, *could* spot us?"

They shove the safe into the back seat of the blue car. "That's what Lonnie's for," Whistle says.

Lonnie chuckles. The switchblade he pulls from his back pocket glints as he walks in front of the car headlights. He's polishing it on his shirtsleeve.

"We've all got skills," Whistle says. "I'm the brains. Lonnie's the muscle."

"What am I?" Sparky asks. His voice squeaks at the end, and Lonnie snorts.

"You're in a bit of a probationary period. Right now," Whistle says, "best I can say is that you're useful."

Sparky twists, glaring toward the coop, and I drop lower from the little window even though I know it's too dark for him to see me. Lonnie pushes past him, knocking his shoulder.

The switchblade isn't in his hand anymore. Now he's holding a huge lighter, flicking the flame on and off. The other two pull smaller lighters from their pockets and follow Lonnie back into the house.

I want my mom. The thought slams me so hard, I fall back on my heels. I cram my hands over my mouth as smoke pours from the house a minute later. The men laugh as they run from it, their arms filled with bags of clothes and electronics. I lift my T-shirt over my nose as more smoke drifts our way. Will the fire spread here, to the chicken coop? It's about fifty yards from the house. Can fire jump?

Gerty doesn't move. Beside the black silhouette of her head, orange glows from inside the house. I hear a door slam shut and then a car engine roaring to life. Gerty stays stationed at the window, not moving a muscle as the men drive away. Every noise makes me jump, but the chickens don't react at all. Neither does Gerty. I clamp my fists over my ears, wedging the Pulaski between my leg and arm, and bite my kneecap to keep from screaming.

We wait for a few seconds, which stretch to years, and then Gerty is yanking my hand. "C'mon, Hayes." She pushes my hand around the Pulaski.

I follow her out of the coop. I wince at the flames licking up from the shattered windows to the outside of the cabin.

"What are you doing?" Gerty screams as I move toward the house.

I flip the Pulaski in my hand and slam it into the dirt, shovel side down, dragging it back again and again to build a trench. "We've got to keep it from getting to the woods," I tell her. Jacey's words at Grandma Louise's about Mom throwing down a line come back to me. "Clear anything that can burn to the dirt level!"

"No, we've got to run!" she screams back.

But the fox is in the woods. The chickens are sleeping behind us. And Rabbit is on the other side of this mountain. I don't stop.

Weren't you terrified?

Always.

"Fine!" Gerty snaps. She disappears into the coop and comes back out with the shovel. She stands with her back toward me, and we dig in opposite directions. She holds the shovel between her left shoulder and neck and uses her foot to push it into the dirt, her right arm still in the sling against her side. Her pace is slower than mine, but I think the homeowners must've raked the yard before they left, because there is only a sparse layer of dried grass to clear. Our trench is a couple of feet wide. Is that enough to stop the flames?

I should've asked Mom more questions. I should've asked for anything she wanted to share. My hands are slick on the handle, and I don't know if it's from sweat or burst blisters.

Embers spark from the house, sizzling the blades of grass beside me. *Focus. Take stock.* I hear the words in Gerty's voice over the rumbling roar of the flames.

We carve a line across the yard between the house and the

coop. There's a gravel driveway from the house to the road, and I think that'll stop the flames on that side. I keep the path going to the flat patch of garden dirt on the other side of the house. I don't know if what we've done will stop the fire, but maybe it will.

Massive black clouds unfurl from the chimney, from shattered windows, and now from the walls on the kitchen side of the house. My lungs feel like wrung-out washcloths, and I don't know if it's from the shoveling or the smoke. Something pops with a loud bang inside the house, and both Gerty and I drop to the ground. The fire gnaws at the grass beside the house now.

I step back. It has to be enough. My arms can't lift the Pulaski again. I rub at my face with my dirty T-shirt. The house is burning so bright that I can see the chickens inside the coop. Flaming ash the size of a dinner plate floats over the trench. It lands on the wooden roof of the coop, singeing out a black smudge. A breeze picks up, and suddenly smoke and flame are a tentacle, stretching toward the little structure. The trench isn't going to hold back what can fly over it. While the embers might sizzle out on the raked lawn, they'll spark and enflame the coop.

More burning ash lands on the sides.

"No!" Gerty comes out of the coop, a chicken under her arm. She throws it onto the grass and then grabs another and another. "Go!" she screams at them. "Go! You can't stay here. *Go!*" But each bird pushes past her, between her legs and back into the coop. The birds are screeching.

"They're going to burn!" Gerty says. Already the wood chips and hay in the chicken run are smoldering. "Why do they keep running inside like this? Can't they tell it's not safe?"

I'm so tired. My arms weigh a thousand pounds. My lungs are too scorched to pull in smoky air. An ember lands near a chicken, and it squawks as it runs over it, back into the building about to burn. The door to the coop was open; I realize the owners probably tried and failed to get the chickens to leave when they did. *Safe as houses.* "They won't go. It's where they live," I say, my tongue tasting the words like ash. "They think it's safe."

Gerty is wailing, and I know it's not because of the chickens. "You have to leave! You have to, even when you don't want to!"

I pick up the Pulaski again. The muscles in my neck bunch as I bring the ax side into the corner of the coop. I swing it again and again until the post snaps. Is this how Mom felt when she fought the duffer?

Gerty chases the chickens into the woods as I ram into the coop with my shoulder, knocking it to the ground, throwing the pieces away from the barrier we created. "Go!" she screams at the birds. "Go!"

The light from the burning house flashes in the eyes of the fox at the edge of the woods.

22

GERTY

Hayes trudges along the road, eyes locked on the distance. "They're going to come," he says. "Rescue workers are going to see the smoke and come out here."

"They won't," I tell him. Or maybe I just think it, because he doesn't even turn. The house burned too fast, too late at night, and, thanks to us, didn't spread into the woods. We've been walking for about an hour and haven't seen another house. No one would've noticed. The sun is starting to rise. The sky looks like cotton candy, like nothing bad ever happened.

Extreme stress triggers extraordinary feats. People have super strength. They've lifted entire cars off their trapped children, yanked doors straight off the hinges, fought in wars for hours. Alex told me a story about a kid who battled a grizzly bear with a pocketknife and won.

Adrenaline is the first spark—it pumps through the

body, dilating air passages to let oxygen flow into muscles. Then the rest of the body steps up. Blood vessels swell, pouring blood into the heart and lungs. Endorphins flood the body, making a person able to keep going long past when adrenaline fades.

But when the crisis ends, the body pays the price. That's what's happening to me. Light-headedness is a normal consequence of an adrenaline rush. So are chills. Exhaustion.

That's what's happening to me, I tell myself again, even as my arm flares in pain. Sometimes pain is helpful. Sometimes it helps a person focus.

I heard what Whistle said. We're in Marystown. That means we're closer than I thought. Pando is nearby. We've nearly made it. I could still have the chance to sit under a single tree, press my spine against its trunk, and know its roots tie into something larger and more ancient than I could imagine (and I'm really good at imagining stuff).

I'll never know what it's like to be so permanent, so anchored. Everything I count on can crumble in a flame, in a crash, in a night. My dad trained me to stand on my own. To *not* count on anyone or anything to hold me up.

But maybe, if we kept going just a little longer, I could see what that would be like.

"*Pando* is Latin for 'I spread,'" I tell Hayes. He doesn't answer. "We're near his borders. We're so close."

"It's just some trees," he says. But that isn't true, and he knows it. "There's something ahead."

We keep moving, our footsteps crunching on the gravel. But somehow we both know to leave the road. We're on the border of Marystown, a huge church parking lot in front of us. Red Cross signs are all around. We made it. I should be happy. We should be clutching each other and smiling and running ahead, but both Hayes and I duck behind trees before the clearing. There's a circle of RVs parked outside the temporary shelter.

We make our way through the woods. At the edge of the parking lot, Hayes reaches out and grabs my hand. He leans the Pulaski against a tree trunk and squeezes my fingertips. We walk out together.

The workers and refugees swarm, everyone hustling. Everyone is moving, doing, prepping. No one has noticed that Hayes and I don't belong to anyone. We look just like everyone else—lost, tired, and scared. Hayes nudges us toward a man with a clipboard and badge. The man lowers a cell phone he has been holding to his ear and then stands on a chair. "Listen up," he says, his voice booming. "We knew this was a temporary fix, too close to the border of the evacuation zone. We need to leave within the hour. We're officially dealing with two fires, the Bryce Canyon wildfire and a new one set in town. That one's mostly under control—contained to one neighborhood—but a little too close for comfort. We'll have a new shelter at the high school in Phillipsburg." People in the crowd murmur. A few groan.

"What do you mean, 'a new one *set* in town'?" a woman asks as she steps down the stairs from her RV. She's wearing a robe and clutching a travel mug. Most people ignore her, continuing with their tasks. But a teenage boy strides toward her. He's holding a paper cup of something steamy. Cocoa, maybe? My tongue twitches, remembering the rich chocolate. Was it really only a few hours ago that we sat on that couch and pretended we were safe?

"I let you sleep in, Ma," the boy says. Hayes and I edge closer to catch his words. He points to the church building, where more people swarm in and out, with his chin. "They're saying those missing kids did it."

"When they crashed their plane? Did they find them?" The woman covers her mouth with her hand.

The boy shakes his head. "Nah. These guys came in for food. They said they heard the kids wanted to be heroes, but when they couldn't get to the Bryce Canyon fire, they set one here so they could say they put it out. Only it got out of hand."

The mother rears back. "How horrible!"

The teen snorts. "Yeah, apparently they're pretty wild kids. Parents are criminals or something. Remember Pete? His little brother, Jaxson, goes to school with them. The boy beat up Jaxson last week for winning a gaga game! They're in a world of trouble. A cop was here looking for them and everything."

"Here?" The woman backsteps up to the RV entrance. "What if they start another fire?"

The teen shrugs. "Rescue workers are putting up flyers with the kids' pictures in shelters all over the place. The cop, he says they're not dangerous."

"Sure, except for burning down half the state." The woman sighs. "Unbelievable. What's wrong with kids today? It's all those video games, I tell you."

"Oh, come on, Ma," the teen groans. They start bickering, and Hayes reaches out and lifts the hood of my sweatshirt over my head.

I droop my shoulders, keeping my gaze on the ground. Both of us back up as though the teen's words were a new fire to escape. Hayes's grip on my hand is painful, crunching my fingers together.

"Hey!" someone behind us calls. Neither of us pauses. "Hey, kids! Don't go running off! We've got to get out of here soon. Get back to your folks."

Hayes lifts his hand like a wave, and we quickly turn to the right, as though heading back into the building. We pass a table filled with fast-food breakfast sandwiches. Hayes grabs a couple and a bottle of water, tucking them against his ribs rather than dropping my hand. Instead of going into the building, we veer to left at the last moment toward the woods. Everything in me wants to sprint—and Hayes is pulling me along in nearly a jog—but I yank on his arm. "Calm down," I whisper. "If we run, we'll draw more attention."

Hayes doesn't look up or at me, but he squeezes my fingers in acknowledgment. He doesn't pause as he reaches out, clutching the Pulaski, as we pass by the tree trunk on the edge of the woods. We keep going, ducking into the trees. Sirens blare behind us and his fingers flex. "Keep going," I mutter.

"What are we going to do?" Hayes asks. We ran for a long time, then we jogged, and now we've been walking for what feels like forever. It was probably a couple of hours. Neither of us spoke until now, even when Hayes handed me the crumpled-up wrapped biscuit. His voice is reedy, like panic is seeping into each word.

I lick my lips. I drank half the water in the bottle he nabbed, but I'm already thirsty. The salty egg and bacon biscuit feels like lead in my stomach. "We keep going."

Hayes groans. "They think *we* set the fire, Gerty. No one's going to believe us that it was three strangers! Not after we stole the plane and broke into that house—"

"We didn't steal the plane. It's my plane."

"But we *did* break into the house!" Hayes swings the Pulaski to his other shoulder. "My mom's a felon. Your parents are . . ." He pauses and gestures into the air like that explains who my parents are.

I swallow, the greasy food coating the inside of my mouth.

I'm so tired. I want to sit down and sleep almost as much as I want to keep moving. I don't even know if I'm heading in the right direction. Another broken rule: move with deliberation. We're simply moving, maybe right to the fire. I need to *think*.

"We're going to go to jail, aren't we?" Hayes says. His hands are folding and unfolding, folding and unfolding. "We're going to go to jail. There are police searching for us, and I'm going to go to jail just like—"

"Stop!" I hiss. I do sit down then, tugging on Hayes's sleeve so he has to pause.

"What are you doing?" But he crouches down, lowering his voice. "Did you see something?"

I shake my head. "We didn't steal a plane. It's my plane. It isn't breaking a law to crash a plane." At least, I don't think it is. But Hayes nods, believing me, so I continue. "We didn't break into the house to steal anything. We went through an unlocked door to ask for help."

"But the coop," Hayes says. "We destroyed it."

"We *saved* those chickens. And we stopped the fire from spreading. We didn't do anything wrong."

Something rustles in the trees ahead of us. Hayes and I stiffen, dropping deeper into a crouch. Ahead of us is the fox, a dead chicken hanging from its snout. It pauses for a second, then trots into the woods.

"Okay, maybe we didn't save *all* the chickens," I say.

Hayes's gasp turns into a laugh. And then he's doubled over

laughing. We both are, the sound of it so strange in the woods. Neither of us speaks as our laughter trickles into nothing. Hayes's shoulders shake and I think he might be crying.

"No one's going to believe us," Hayes says. "Maybe eventually they will, but not for a long time. They'll only believe the bad stuff, even if we tell them why we did it. Even if we're sorry." Hayes presses his palms into his legs. "Maybe they'll never forgive us. Maybe they'll only remember the bad forever. That can happen."

He's thinking about his mom. I know that. But maybe he's also talking about Matthew.

"I want to see Pando," I whisper. "I think . . . I think if I see Pando, I can handle it. Whatever happens next."

"That doesn't make any sense," Hayes says. "We need to turn back."

"You heard them, though," I say. "They're already evacuated by now. If we go back, we'll be heading right into the fire zone. They left, and no one's still looking for us there."

"So what do we do?" Hayes whispers.

"We keep going. I know where Marystown is on the map. Pando is north of it." I point ahead. "If we see someone along the way who can help us, we stop. But until then, we keep going."

"If we go back, though, I bet the church has a phone. Even if it's in the fire zone, we can call for help." His dark eyes bore into mine, waiting for me to say why that's a bad idea. But it isn't.

"Do you know that Pando has been around since the last ice age?" I say instead. "How many fires do you think he went through? How many of his trees died?" I can't look at Hayes's eyes anymore, so I gaze over his shoulder instead. "Pando is dying, and no one knows why. They think it might be too many things gnawing at him. Maybe it's that there aren't enough fires anymore. But maybe it's something else."

"Maybe it's all of that." Hayes's voice isn't panicky anymore. Now he sounds tired.

"Maybe," I say. "I just want to see him. Know he's okay. I think . . . I think I'll be okay if I can see him."

And I know, too, that it isn't bravery or friendship or anything noble that makes Hayes nod. It's fear. Neither of us is ready to face the damage we caused.

23

HAYES

A breakfast biscuit and half a bottle of water isn't enough to keep my stomach from twisting itself into knots.

I'd eat another cricket, I really would.

When I'm not thinking about food, I'm figuring out how to tell Gerty my decision.

Here it is: I'm not going back. I'll go with her to Pando and then she'll go back to her parents. But I'm not going home again.

"Home" isn't the right word. Home wasn't a yellow apartment with the ceiling falling like snow. Home wasn't a white kitchen with a huge island for doing homework. Home isn't Grandma Louise with her crates full of critters. Home isn't where your only friend picks up and leaves.

The truth is, I had a home. It was Mom. And she

left. For a long time she couldn't live without those pills. But *I* figured out how to live without her. Now I don't know if I can learn to live with her again. Charlie is better with her. I'm better off on my own.

We hike northward, one step in front of the other. The mountains merge and fold into one another, like a piece of paper God crumpled in his fist. We go around ridges on narrow trails that deer or moose tamped down. Some look wider, as though a dirt bike or ATV might use them. Does that mean we're on the way to a town?

I don't ask Gerty what she's thinking, and she doesn't ask me. Sometimes I forget where we're going. Sometimes she sings. Sometimes I want to go back, but we're too far from anything now.

The sky fades from hazy pink to hazy gray. My lungs don't seem able to pull enough oxygen into them. I watch the horizon for smoke and for flame, but all I see is sage and juniper. We're visible to anyone, but there aren't any roads crossing our path and we don't see anyone. We reach another thick patch of woods at the base of a steep decline. We hear the waterfall before we see it.

Gerty doesn't say a word, doesn't move to unpack her emergency kit for the iodine or flask. Maybe this water is so fast moving, we don't need to worry about bacteria. Maybe we're past worrying about it. I climb a boulder beside the waterfall and push my face into the stream to drink from it. The cold mountain water coats the inside of my chest as though I am also a waterfall ledge. For a moment I think I'm going to be okay.

Gerty doesn't move, so I bring some water to her in my cupped hands. "C'mon, Gerty. You have to drink."

She blinks at me. I hold my hands out to her again. Finally she leans forward. I tip the water into her mouth. Her lips are chapped and cracked. Blood blooms at the corners of her mouth when she opens it.

"Gerty?" She's pale and her eyes are glassy. I press my hand against her forehead. I feel my own forehead to compare. Her skin is scorching hot. The air has been mild all day, not cold and not hot, either. It doesn't make sense that she would be so hot from hiking. This is something else. "Okay. It's okay. We've got to cool you off a little." I loop my arm around her waist. She whimpers and the sound hollows my knees. "You're going to be all right," I tell us both, even as goose bumps pebble my arms.

Using the Pulaski like a walking stick, I hold her upright against my side as we slide along the rocks to where the water empties into a pool before spilling down the rest of the mountain. "You need to cool off a little." Can you get fevers from dehydration? I don't know. I don't know anything.

Gerty unzips her hoodie and shrugs out her good arm. I unknot the sling we made from the ultralight fabric and free her other arm. She winces, keeping it cradled against her side.

"Help me?" she asks, and I'm so relieved to hear her speak that my chin wobbles.

It's nearly evening, but there's still enough light for me to see that her injured arm looks all wrong. The bandage is soaked through with a brownish-yellow crust, and the skin is puffy and red. A streak of red like a marker line runs up three inches from where the hinge was embedded, toward her shoulder. "It's bad, isn't it?" Gerty says, her voice hoarse.

"It's not so bad," I say, but my voice is shaky and ruining everything.

"Maybe if I just wash it," she says.

I nod and help her to the water's edge. Gerty leans forward and splashes water up over her face. It trickles down her arm. Part of me is surprised it doesn't sizzle when it hits the inflamed skin. "That feels good," she says. "We should splash more in the stream, don't you think? Remember that time we danced in the middle? I think he would've liked that we did that."

She isn't talking to me, I realize when she holds up her hand to watch the water dribble from her fingertips.

"Gerty, I think you're pretty sick."

She leans forward, her knees dipping into the water, and brings more up to her mouth to drink. "Hayes." This time when she looks at me, her eyes are focused. "My dad isn't looking for me. He would've found me."

"You don't know that," I tell her. "I'm sure they're all looking for us. I bet Nanny Pat's in the sky."

She shakes her head. "I miss him."

"Your dad?"

"Him too." She drinks more water, then puts her wet hand on the back of her neck. After a few minutes she stands, wobbling on her feet. "Let's go."

I fill the flask and add three drops of the iodine, even though I guess that doesn't make a lot of sense anymore, and then loop my arm around her waist. "We're almost there," she says. But I know the truth.

We're running out of time.

We walk faster when we leave the waterfall. Gerty is shivering, even though it feels comfortable outside. Does that mean she's still running a fever? Grandma Louise says fevers are the way bodies fight off infection. Maybe this is a sign she's getting better? I know I'm lying to myself, but I let the thought loop around my mind anyway.

A dirt path wends from the edge of the woods. I follow it, even though I'm not positive that it flows northward. The path widens. Maybe it leads to a road. A cow moos in the distance. If there are cows around, people must be too, right?

We're probably past the evacuation zone—back at the church, the Red Cross person said they were just inside the border. There are narrow tracks in the dirt, not large enough for car tires but maybe an ATV. I glance at Gerty, waiting for her to redirect us, but her eyes are barely open as she pushes ahead. "Gerty?"

"I think I might've thought I knew more than I did," she mutters.

I can't help it; I laugh. "Yeah, that happens to me sometimes."

"Maybe my dad thinks he knows more than he does too." She stumbles and I catch her. I wince, realizing I grabbed her sore arm, but she doesn't react to the pressure. I don't think it's because it's getting better. "Alex wants me to be strong enough not to need him. But he's my dad."

"You never talk about your brother," I say, trying to keep her focused. I hear something ahead of us. A car engine. Gerty, who notices everything, doesn't seem to hear it.

"That's because I killed him."

I suck in my breath. "No, you didn't," I say.

"The doctors said Matthew had something called SIDS, sudden infant death syndrome. That he stopped breathing in his sleep sometime early that morning. Dad—Alex—he was going to check on Matthew when I woke up before the sun." Her words are as soft as tissue paper but steady. "Only I cried for him to watch cartoons with me, and then when he tried to check on Matthew again, I started whining for breakfast. I didn't want anything in the house, so he went to the store for pancake mix. He said not to wake Mom—Jennifer. To let them both sleep in until he got back." Gerty's eyes drift shut.

"If I hadn't done that, Alex would've checked on him hours earlier. What if Matthew would've woken up? What if he would've lived if it weren't for me?"

"You don't know that." I don't think she hears me. "It's not your fault, Gerty. It would've happened regardless."

"But what if it happened because of me?" She sighs, and the sound rattles like a snake in her chest. "Everything changed after that. They didn't even want me to call them Mom and Dad anymore. They said it was to be more independent, but what if it was because they knew it was my fault?"

"It wasn't," I tell her. "It happened *to* you. To all of you."

She doesn't say anything. I don't think she hears me. So I whisper my secret too. "It's my fault Mom went to jail. I was always wishing she'd be different, be more like the other moms. And then when she tried to make our crappy apartment look like my friend's house, she got hurt. And then I was the one who knocked her pills down the drain. I wrecked everything. I ruined it all."

Light filters through the trees at the bottom of the slight hill we're going down. The path is hard-packed dirt now. Gerty leans against me, and I'm holding her up more than she is standing on her own. Her head dips against my neck, and her face feels too hot. Funny, isn't it, how this is the most scared I've ever been, more scared than when the plane was crashing, when the house was burning, when my mom didn't look back. *Please be okay, Gerty. Please be okay.*

I hear voices. Someone says, "Bring your ATV around. Mine's already on the trailer."

My heart thunders in my chest; somehow Gerty doesn't hear the people packing up their cabin just through the trees.

I'm pulling Gerty along now, her legs barely moving.

Hold on, Gerty. Don't be dead. Please don't be dead. I'm blubbering, my whole body shaking. I realize that her chest is rising and falling. She's breathing. She's alive.

"Hey!" A woman comes out of the house. "Who's there?"

Another woman runs over to me from the garage. "My friend needs help," I say to her without looking up from Gerty. "Her arm. She's hurt. Please help her."

I lower Gerty to the grass and push her hair from her face. The woman squats in front of me. She presses her fingers to Gerty's neck, taking her pulse. "Cassie, call 911!"

I glance behind me. The woman by the house, Cassie, already has the phone pressed to her ear. "I'm sorry," I whisper to Gerty.

"I can't get through," Cassie says. "I'll keep trying, but let's get her to the ranger station in Fishlake. They'll know what to do."

"She needs water," I say. "Food too. We haven't eaten anything in a while."

Cassie runs over and the two women lift Gerty, then lay her on the back seat of their truck. Cassie calls for help again and again, even as she closes the hitch on the truck and gets in the driver's seat. The other woman turns off the ATV, tosses the key into the bag attached behind the seat, and zips it shut. She leaves it as she darts toward the truck.

"Get in the truck, kid. We've got to go!"

I stumble backward, into the woods.

"Let's go!" the woman yells as she gets into the truck. She shakes her head in my direction and shuts the door. Cassie shifts into drive, and the truck peels out of the driveway into the dark.

I stand in front of the ATV. I know they left it behind so they could get Gerty to help as quickly as possible, but it feels like a gift. A helmet is on the back, and I strap it on my head. I take the key out of the bag attached to the seat. I wait for someone to stop me, but there isn't anyone around. I sit on the seat. My foot presses on the gas, and I cut the wheel so the vehicle spins to the side. I go a few feet and then take my foot off the gas.

This, I know, is wrong. Maybe Gerty's right and everything we did before now was just a mistake. But *this* is wrong. I'm breaking the law.

My truth from earlier echoes through me. *I wrecked everything. I ruined it all.* I find the headlights and flip them on, then take off down the path.

I'm sorry for leaving you, Gerty.

I'm not going back.

The lights from the ATV are dim. There isn't any other traffic. Eyes flash in the dark. I know it can't be the same fox, but it feels like a good sign anyway. The compass on the dashboard of the ATV says I'm heading north. Almost there. Almost *where*?

The dream of a burning ocean comes back to me every time I close my eyes. Every choice I've made, every step I've taken, everything is about to burn around me.

When I open my eyes, the inky black seems to swallow me whole. The road narrows and turns to stone and then dirt. The ATV beeps, and a light I don't understand flashes on the dashboard. Soon the engine keens. I veer off the road. The engine sputters and then stops altogether, the gas tank empty. I push the ATV behind a tree so no one steals it. A basket on the back has a blanket and some beef jerky. I sink down and make myself chew the jerky slowly. I leave the headlights on.

I don't like the dark. Mom used to keep the door cracked when she put us to bed at night. She said it was so she could hear if we needed anything. But I think she knew that triangle of yellow light made me feel safe. I can't see any of the stars now. My head throbs almost as much as my stomach.

A breeze rolls over the hill, and I pull the blanket over my shoulders tighter. I tilt my head back against the rubber of the tire. I need to rest for a little. Then I'll keep going until I see Pando. Gerty said she'd be okay if she could see it. Maybe she'll be okay if *I* see it. Maybe I'll be all right too.

Maybe after that I'll know what to do next.

24

CHIEF SKIP

None of this adds up.

Skip has met these kids. He knows them. They got a raw deal, both of them, in the trauma department, but they're loved. They're not runners. Are they?

It's been three days and nights. Their chance of being found alive lowers every hour. Crews are combing through the woods. The fire is slowly being contained. Still, nothing.

The phone on his desk rings, and he answers before it finishes the first peal. "This is Marystown municipal officer Peters," the caller says. His voice is as slow moving as the crime in the region. "We identified another house fire. Clearly set, like the one that took out two residences and a few acres of brush. But this one . . . it's peculiar."

"How so?" asks Skip, his heart thumping.

"I'm sending through some images. Check your email."

Almost immediately Skip's desktop computer pings. He clicks on the attachments. "Tell me what I'm looking at, Peters."

"The house was filled with an accelerant. Still running tests, but we think it's gasoline."

"What makes you say that?"

"The perps weren't too bright. They left three empty jugs at the scene, tossed in the driveway. I think they were confident the fire would melt them down."

"But that didn't happen," Skip prods.

Peters chuckles. "Nah. Something or someone . . . someones maybe . . . made sure it didn't spread. Saved us all a world of trouble, chunking a line around the yard so the fire sizzled out. Even knocked the bejeezus out of the chicken coop and tossed the pieces away from the house."

Skip zooms in on the line of turned-over earth circling the house. "What would it take to make a perimeter like that, Peters?"

"Well, now, I'm no firefighter, but the chief there, he says a shovel or Pulaski would do the job. Said it looked near professional."

"So not something a couple kids could do?"

Peters breathes heavily into the phone. "Nah, I suspect not. But it's peculiar, like I said."

"Give me that location?"

Skip drums his finger on the spot on the map with the strange fire.

He's thinking about Hayes, about the kid's face when he stopped by to tell Tara and Louise about the thefts nearby. The kid was terrified of being in trouble. And Gerty? A kid who lives off the land wouldn't set a fire. Would she know how to put one out, though? Tara still hasn't found her Pulaski.

He looks again at the map, at the radius of where the plane might've crashed, and drums his fingers again. The Marystown fire is on the northern edge of that radius.

If only he knew what the kids were thinking.

He folds the map, shoves it into his pocket, and grabs his keys.

Chief Skip leans forward, his elbows on Mrs. Freid's desk.

"I've been racking my brain for days over this," the guidance counselor says. "It's why I'm here now, two hours before school starts, combing through my notes."

"Any conclusions?" Skip asks.

Mrs. Freid nods. "Despite their past experiences, I don't think they ran away." Her eyes flick to Tara, who is seated to Skip's right, her arms tightly crossed and her jaw set. The fierce mom keeps pace beside him nearly everywhere he goes. When he stormed from his office to head to the school, map in hand, she was already waiting in the lobby, though it was barely five in the morning. Once they find Hayes, he hopes she'll stick around for other reasons. Though hopefully without the panicked posture and dark circles under her eyes.

"Of course they ran." Nanny Pat sighs from her perch at the edge of the seat on his left. Her constant presence isn't quite as welcome in Skip's life. She, too, was waiting in the lobby, but Skip had a feeling the older woman typically beat the sun at rising. "They got into a plane and literally flew away."

Mrs. Freid shakes her head. "They left. But we're making the leap that it was to run away. What if they fully intended to come back?"

"But Hayes took my Pulaski," Tara says. Her voice is hoarse.

Mrs. Freid looks at her lap. "Have you considered that he took it so you couldn't?"

Tara goes perfectly still, the blood draining from her face. Skip gives her a moment to speak. When she doesn't, he says, "Explain."

Mrs. Freid swallows and slowly raises her eyes to lock with his. "Hayes talked about a dream he had. It was the first time he truly opened up. He was running toward a fire, one the size of an ocean, but the faster he ran, the farther away it got."

Nanny Pat gasps. "So they *are* going to the fire. That horrible boy convinced my granddaughter to run toward a fire!"

Skip doesn't know what's more surprising—Tara's strangled sob or Mrs. Freid's burst of laughter. "Convinced? *Gerty?*" The counselor hiccups. "When has anyone successfully convinced Gerty to do anything she didn't want to do?" Mrs. Freid wipes her hand over her mouth, reinstating her serious face. "Right.

The fire is in a dream. It's not literal. I think the fire is . . ." She gestures toward Tara.

Mrs. Freid leans toward Tara until she makes and keeps eye contact. "He wants a relationship with you again and is terrified he won't have the chance to build it. He's scared of losing you. Does that sound like someone who would run?"

Nanny Pat snorts. "You shrinks always think it's the mother." She plucks up the framed picture of Mrs. Freid with her mother from the bookshelf beside her. Somehow a tree is below them in the background.

Mrs. Freid sighs. "I'm in Middle-of-Nowhere, Utah. Know why? It's about the only place where I can be sure my mom won't pop in to tell me about how she ran into my ex-husband at Whole Foods. So, yes, I do usually think it's the mother."

Skip rubs the back of his neck. "None of this insight tells us where they went. Did they mention a location? A place that's important to them?"

Mrs. Freid stares at the framed picture. Then she flips furiously through her notes. "A tree. I thought Gerty was messing around at first when she told me about her tree, giving me the name of an animal instead. Panda."

"Pando," Skip corrects.

"Yes, that's it!" Mrs. Freid exclaims. "Gerty said that's why she wanted to be in CAP, so she could see Pando."

"She knew her parents were leaving," Nanny Pat breaks in. "She must have wanted to see it before she left."

This is the best part of his job, when the bread-crumb clues form a path he can follow. This one leads to two kids headed toward 106 acres of protected forestland. He stands, pulls the map from his back pocket, and spreads it atop Mrs. Freid's desk in one fluid movement. Then he snags a red Sharpie from the cup of pens on her desk and circles a section of land in Fishlake. "*This* is Pando."

25

HAYES

A huffing noise wakes me.

My head is still tilted back on the tire. I open my eyes to a royal-blue sky. Almost morning. My neck is so sore that tipping my head forward to see the source of the sound feels like I'm ripping the muscles.

Another huff. The fox is by my ankle, sniffing at the packet of beef jerky. I startle, kicking my legs, and he runs off, the package in his mouth. It couldn't be the same fox, right?

I push to my feet and, just in case, try the ATV again. The engine doesn't turn at all. The headlights don't even glimmer. The battery must be dead too. I strap the helmet to the back, feeling a little silly about having worn it all night. "Can you believe I did that?" I say to Gerty, my tongue like sandpaper in my sawdust mouth.

I shake my head. Gerty isn't with me. When was the

last time I had something to drink? The waterfall. It wasn't that long ago. My stomach gurgles. I remember that I put more water in the flask. But the emergency kit was strapped to Gerty's back.

The sky is lightening to the east, so I turn left, hoping Pando is still in that direction. Everything hurts. Will it forever? I remember how drinking from the waterfall felt like it was pouring inside me too. Maybe I'll be thirsty forever. I'm not hungry anymore, though. A part of me knows I should be worried about that. I should be starving. But I'm empty.

Maybe I'll never get to Pando.

Look, Hayes. Look!

Maybe I'll be like the Mother of the Forest, an ugly reminder of everything that hurts. Maybe I'll wear my anger forever, make everyone else see it, make them regret.

Feelings are temporary, Hayes. Gerty is whispering in my ear, even though I left her behind. She'll never forgive me for that, will she? I left her.

Another step. Another.

Charlie won't forgive me either. I left him, too. I let him get hurt and then I left him. How can he believe that I love him when I did that? You don't leave people you care about. I open my eyes, and for a moment I think I see him, his eye still purple. I blink and he's gone.

Fire killed the Mother of the Forest. It charred her because she didn't have the bark that should've protected her. When it was ripped away, nothing could keep her safe from the flames. But the truth is, she would've died anyway without the bark to hold her together.

Sometimes I think I'm the tree and Mom's the bark.

Look, Hayes! Look!

Sometimes she's the tree, and I'm clawing at everything that holds her together just so she remembers I'm there.

I whisper my secret into the dawn. "I wrecked everything. I ruined it all." Mom is back, but we're still in pieces because of me, because I can't stop being angry. Why can't I stop being angry?

Look, Hayes! Look!

I do, finally tearing my eyes off my feet and the thoughts I'm stomping into the ground. The sun is rising. Pinks and blues swirl like cotton candy. Stretching in front of me are aspen trees, all their leaves the same shade of green, all of them with narrow white trunks, black shapes on them like eyes gazing back at me in the dawn.

Pando.

26

CHIEF SKIP

Skip stands behind his desk, plotting his next steps.

The good news: he has a potential location where the kids are heading. The bad news? Every minute that area overlaps more with the fire evacuation zone. The worse news: apparently his policing is now done via committee, considering both Tara and Nanny Pat are simultaneously telling him what to do.

"I can't," Skip says, and takes a step back at the fury on Nanny Pat's and Tara's faces at those two little words. "I can't in good conscience let you head into an evacuation zone!"

"I'm a trained firefighter. I *know* what I'm getting into," Tara snaps, her eyes narrowed.

Nanny Pat nods in approval at Tara. "I might be an old woman, but I'm an experienced rescuer. Don't think you're stopping either one of us, Chief."

Skip dimly realizes the irksome sound in his ears is his own gnashing teeth. "Listen, I need you to—"

"Howdy, folks!" All three of them turn as a young man, who barely looks out of high school despite sporting full fire-fighting gear, steps into the room. "I'm Hank. Me and my engine, we're on loan to the region. Wondering if you could direct me toward Fishlake? I'm supposed to relieve a fire engine there, and there's no GPS signal here, and, well . . ." His face flushes deep red. "Turns out I'm not so great at read-ing a map."

Tara shoots a grin at Skip that stops his heart and then says, "I'll show you the way, Hank. I was just about to hitch up with the fire camp crew myself."

"All right!" Hank says at the same time Skip barks at her to hold on.

Tara darts after Hank, grabbing his arm and turning him out of the office as Nanny Pat, surprisingly spritely for her age, jumps to her feet, blocking Skip's path. "Now, Skip, what's the plan? At least tell me you've mobilized the local CAP."

Skip's cell phone rings. Tara pauses in the doorway with Hank, and Nanny Pat sucks in her breath as he answers. They're all aware that every call could be the news they're wait-ing for or the news they're dreading. He swallows as he listens. He absorbs the words, eyes flicking to the map on his desk, and then nods. "Got it. I'll . . . I'll let them know."

He hangs up. He turns to face Nanny Pat. "They found

Gerty. She was transferred from Fishlake Community via ambulance to the hospital in Salt Lake City late last night. Broken arm, dehydrated, in and out of consciousness, but alive. Finally gave the docs her name this morning."

Nanny Pat pales. She nods. "I'll get Jennifer."

He lifts his head to face Tara, who is frozen in place by what he hasn't said. This is the worst part of his job. "Hayes?" she whispers as she moves back toward his desk.

Skip strides to stand beside her. He grabs her hand and squeezes it. "Hayes is the one who brought her out of the woods." He points to a spot on the map. "Here. The cabin where he got her help is here."

"He's there? He's safe?" Joy radiates through Tara, and Skip has a flash of the person she used to be, the one she might someday be again. And then he utters words he knows will banish that ghost. "He ran. The couple took Gerty to the hospital, got home and saw their ATV was missing."

"He ran." Tara wobbles on her feet, and Skip moves his grip to hold her upright by the elbow.

"We'll find him." He drums his finger on the spot on the map again. "I'm going to go to the hospital to interview Gerty, get a better perspective on how he is and where he's headed. But if he is still going to Pando, this is the direction he'd be heading."

"He's going to Pando," Tara says. She leans into Skip for just a second and then steps backward. "Let me know how she is and what she tells you about Hayes. Hank's going to give me a lift to Fishlake, and then I'm going to find my son."

Nanny Pat squeezes Tara's shoulder as she passes. "I'll let local CAP leaders know you're on the way."

27

GERTY

The sheets on the bed are crisp and white.

A blackbird bursts into the cockpit, twitching on the dashboard as Hayes screams.

The gown I'm wearing is thin but soft. The light through the window is bright.

My hands and the gear stick are one, cemented together in fear. Hayes wraps his arms around me as we plummet.

The needle in my arm is so sharp, I don't feel it, even as it opens into a vein, filling it with nutrients and medicine.

Fire surrounds us, lapping against the border of dirt we carve. My arm is a flame. I am burning, inside out.

My arm is wrapped in a cast and tucked against my chest. I'm safe. I'm safe. I'm safe.

I open my eyes. Nanny Pat is sitting beside me. Chief Skip slowly stands from a chair at the edge of the room. Hayes. He isn't there. *Where is he?*

I close my eyes again.

Ash around me. Flames inside me. Everything fades.

"Hayes!" I call. But when I open my eyes this time, I remember. I'm in the hospital. Hayes left me.

Nanny Pat squeezes my hand. "Stay with us now, Gerty." I nod, and she smiles. "That's my girl."

Chief Skip clears his throat. No one else is there. Nanny Pat squeezes my hand again, and I know not to ask for Alex and Jennifer.

They left me too.

"You gave us quite a scare," Skip says. He squats beside the bed, so we're eye to eye.

"Hayes said we're going to go to jail."

Skip winces. "I'm not keen on the idea of arresting kids. We've got a lot of questions that need answers. I'm going to start with the most important one."

"We didn't mean to break into the house," I blurt. Skip holds up his hand, but I need to tell him the truth. "We wanted to get inside so we could call for help. I swear. The door was unlocked. I'll pay them back for the cocoa. I will! The whistling guy, he's the one who broke in, he and the other two guys." My words tremble at the way Skip's jaw clenches, but I have to get this out before I float away again. "They're the ones who started the fire. We saved the chickens and the fox and the woods and—"

Skip breaks in, "I want to know all of this, I do. But right now we need to make sure Hayes is safe. I doubt his condition is a heck of a lot better than yours." Skip's eyes dart around my face and my arm. He swallows. "Where is Hayes?"

What does it mean to be loyal?

"He's going to Pando," I whisper.

Skip nods. "Is he hurt?"

I wrecked everything. I ruined it all.

I shake my head. He pulls in a big breath and nods. Skip stands, the phone already pressed against his ear as he strides from the room. "I'll be back in a minute, Gerty."

Nanny Pat clears her throat. "You broke your promise to me."

I don't look at her, staring instead at the white blanket under my fingers. "I'm sorry."

She lets out a big breath. Her footsteps click across the linoleum floor as she takes Skip's place to stand beside me. "It's going to take a lot of work to build back trust between us."

Anger flares through me. "I'm sure you have conditions."

Suddenly her fingers, cool and soft, brush my cheek as she sits down in the chair next to me. "Don't shut me out," she says. "That's the only condition." The anger turns to smoke. I feel wetness on my forehead as a tear drops from her chin. "I lost a grandson and then a daughter. Please, Gerty, I don't want to lose you, too."

"They're not coming back, are they?" I whisper.

Nanny Pat's fingers rest on my shoulder, above the cast. They send shivers down my back. I don't ever remember her holding my hand or hugging me. I try not to lean into the touch. It's been a long time since anyone hugged me. "You don't know that. When I told Jennifer you were here, she went to find Alex."

Nanny Pat must not have gotten a lot of sleep lately, because after just a couple of minutes, she's snoring, her hand still on my shoulder, tangled in my messy hair.

Someone softly knocks on the door. Nanny Pat doesn't stir, even as Mrs. Freid walks inside.

I sneer at her. *Feelings are temporary.* But they're not. Sometimes feelings twist and tunnel. Sometimes they wrap themselves into every bit of a person, locking them into a place where nothing else can grow.

Survivors shouldn't feel sorry for themselves. Pity serves no purpose and survival depends on moving with intention. *Focus. Take stock.* So what if Alex, Jennifer, and Lilith left? I have what I need. Being sad serves no purpose.

Mrs. Freid pulls up a chair on the other side of the bed, the metal legs screeching across the floor and making Nanny Pat snort in her sleep. She opens her eyes, blearily looks at us, and closes them again. She doesn't move her hand from where it rests in my hair and along my shoulder. Mrs. Freid doesn't say anything as she folds her hands on her lap.

"Hayes left me," I say.

Mrs. Freid nods. "Your grandmother phrased it differently

when I called. She said the doctors told her you wouldn't have lasted much longer before the sepsis, that means 'blood infection'—"

"I know what 'sepsis' means."

Mrs. Freid's mouth twitches for a moment, but she continues. Her voice is steady and low. "Well, that's what was affecting your arm, more so than the fracture. If Hayes hadn't gotten you to help when he did, you might not have recovered. He *saved* you."

I shake my head. I could've kept going.

"What's so important about Pando?" Her voice is calm, curious. "What made you risk so much to see it?"

I bury my cheek against Nanny Pat's hand and block out everything but the thoughts that thunder in my head. I was so close. I wanted to be part of something bigger. I wanted to stand on roots and know they tied into everything around me. But Mrs. Freid won't understand that. No one will.

I thought she would leave once I turned away from her, but Mrs. Freid continues as though we were having a conversation rather than simply her talking to me. "After you shared your thoughts on *my* tree, I put aside my usual reading material." She shifts in the seat, making it squeak again. "I've been reading about trees. How they communicate."

I peek back at her. She smiles. I tuck my head back down. Nanny Pat sighs but doesn't wake. Her fingers flex and tangle further in my hair.

"You were right." She laughs when I snort. Of course I was right. "Trees *do* communicate. It appears individual trees can be lonely, or at least *not* lonely. Ones with roots that overlap with others seem healthier, live longer. Want to hear something I found particularly interesting in my reading?"

She pauses. I shrug with my good shoulder. "Some trees drop their seeds right under them. They'll keep the seedlings in their own shadow, ensuring they grow slowly but strongly. Wayward seedlings will shoot up too fast and spindly, likely to fall over. But the ones whose roots are closer will be strong enough when the matriarch—that means 'mother'—"

"I know what 'matriarch' means."

"When the matriarch topples, those seedlings will be strong enough to soar in the sunlight."

Pando doesn't use just seeds. He sends up shoots from the roots, called sproutings. I'll tell her about that another time, though. Right now I'm ignoring her. But then I realize something. She's trying to trick me. "Is this supposed to be some sort of analogy?"

Mrs. Freid laughs. "You tell me. But I'm not done yet. What I found truly interesting was that trees' roots often keep nourishing fallen trees around them, sending food resources into their roots, even though their trunks are damaged or even simply stumps. The trees around the stumps keep them going, even when they're in what humans would consider grief."

Neither of us speaks for a long time. Then I say, "My parents left me too. I don't think they're coming back." I lift my head and glance over at her.

She nods, her jaw flexing. "Your family has been through a lot of painful experiences." I realize she knows about Matthew. Both of us are silent. I think she's going to leave when she bends over to her bag, but instead she pulls out a book with a tree on the cover. Soon the only sound is her finger running down the right side of her book as she turns the pages.

"We don't talk about him. It's like he was never there," I say.

Mrs. Freid's finger pauses on its journey down the page. "Lots of people try to disconnect from grief. It doesn't work, does it?"

I close my eyes, pretending to sleep, and she continues to sit there.

"Why don't they love me as much as they loved him?" I whisper into the quiet.

Mrs. Freid breathes out and in. "I don't think love has anything to do with it. I think it's pain. Theirs casts too big of a shadow, and not the kind that allows for growth."

My cheeks burn when tears leak from my closed eyes. Mrs. Freid's hand curls around mine. It's sort of like having roots, her fingers overlapping mine and Nanny Pat's in my hair.

28

SPARKY

Lonnie leans against the side of the car next to Sparky as he calls his brother. Whistle waits behind the wheel, pulling up directions to Wyoming on his phone. That's where they'll head next, he says, after they find just one more job.

Sparky doesn't point out that the last job was supposed to be the *last* one. So was the one before that.

The phone rings and rings. "I'm telling you," Sparky says, "Skip's real busy. The fires, the missing kids—"

"Kid," Lonnie says. Whistle got an alert on his phone that one of the kids had been found, which is why they've cut this would-be final job short after quick grabs of jewelry, clothes, and electronics, stacked in the trunk of the car. They headed south, taking a side road to sneak past a fire engine. They were close enough to the fire that Sparky wanted to argue when Lonnie pulled the gas can from the back seat. What was the point? The air was thick with smoke. They could see the glow of the flames from the windows of the house. But Lonnie said they had to do it right.

So they lit that house and took off.

Whistle didn't laugh at the irony a few minutes later, when the gas light of the car flashed on as they were detoured by a different fire engine blocking the road. He pulled over to look for new routes and ordered Sparky to get the lowdown from his brother on whether the police were going to be a problem.

Sparky swallows against a sudden flood of spit in his mouth as he hears his brother's voice on the line, telling him to leave a message. "Voice mail," he says, and presses the end button.

Lonnie curses. "What kind of guy doesn't answer his brother's call?"

"One who has a brother like me," Sparky says.

Lonnie squints at him. "So many things wrong with you, Sparky. Why you adding self-esteem issues to the list?"

Sparky blinks back.

"On the other hand," Lonnie says, "if he somehow suspected you, he definitely would've picked up."

Sparky's phone vibrates in his pocket; it must be Skip calling back. He doesn't pick up, and works to keep his face smooth. He saw those two kids run for the coop, but did they spot him? How much did they hear? Could they make him and the others? He swallows again, remembering how Whistle said his name when they were in the house. Why couldn't he have a name like John or Dave? There probably aren't too many grown men named Sparky.

"You okay, Sparky?" Lonnie asks.

Whistle saves him from answering by ordering them back in the car. "Get in!" Something about his tone makes Sparky look over his shoulder. Behind them looms an avalanche of pitch-black smoke.

"C'mon, c'mon," Whistle mutters, his foot pressing the gas pedal as the car barrels down the road. Sparky keeps his eyes glued to the trees closest to them, trying not to notice that, in the distance, orange flames seem to be pouring like lava across the forest. The path behind them is nothing but smoke. Flames to the side. Forest to the other.

"It's like we're being herded," Lonnie says.

Sparky rears back when a coyote runs from the woods, its tail smoking. The animal limps a few steps and then falls. Sparky tries to breathe, willing the animal to get back up.

But then he loses sight of the coyote as Whistle screams and slams on the brakes. Sparky shoots forward, the seat belt cutting into his shoulder as Lonnie curses in the back seat. Ahead of them is a fire engine. Beside it, a firefighter in full gear and a woman in jeans are frantically waving for them to stop. They run toward the car. Sparky lowers his window to catch the firefighter's words.

"Oh, thank God! We need a jump. Battery's dead. No one is supposed to still be in this area, but man, I'm glad to see you guys!" He backsteps a little to get the jumper cables he dropped when he began waving at them. Sparky's eyes snag on the woman. He knows her; she's the missing kid's mom.

She tilts her head at him. "You're Skip's brother, aren't you?" she says. "I saw you at the station."

Whistle curses under his breath and then pushes Sparky's arm. "Get out," he says to him.

"What?" Sparky gasps.

"She made you," Whistle hisses, spittle flying from his mouth. "Get out of the car." Whistle presses down on Sparky's seat belt button, leans over him, and throws open the door.

"What? They just need help. They don't know anything," he whispers.

"You want to help them? Help them!" He kicks at Sparky's side, pushing him out of the car. Lonnie leans over the back seat, shoving him too.

Sparky rolls from the car as Whistle accelerates around Tara and the firefighter.

The firefighter is young and lanky, scruff sprouting on his chin in uneven patches. He grabs Sparky by the elbow and yanks him to his feet. He doesn't ask why they left him behind. He simply tells Sparky his name is Hank.

Tara nods at Sparky once and then says, "Let's get to work." She strides back to the dead fire engine.

The cloud of black is so thick and so close, Sparky can barely drag air into his lungs. "How? They left us!"

Hank bumps against Sparky's shoulder as they follow Tara. "Three things." He holds up a finger. "One, it probably wouldn't have worked. This bird has three batteries. Would've drained that car for sure, and still might not have been enough." He raises another finger. "Two: they're heading right into the worst of it, so if I were you, I'd rather be here."

"What's three?"

Hank grins. "We can't get anywhere, but this lady came up with a mad plan to keep us safe until the fire passes. If we're going to make it work, we for sure need your help. C'mon."

"Are we going to die?" Sparky asks as the orange in the woods creeps closer.

Hank laughs. "I'm a newbie, but she's an old-timer. And old-timers? They've always got a plan."

"This is a terrible plan," Sparky says a minute later.

Tara's nostrils flare as she narrows her eyes. "Keep a toe in the black and we're good." With that, Tara hands Sparky a red canister with a long handle on the side.

"A fire extinguisher? This isn't going to—"

Tara sighs. "Tell him, Hank."

Hank grins. "That ain't an extinguisher. It's a drip torch. She's going to light it, and then you're going to turn that little screw. It'll let fuel drip onto the wick and dribble onto the ground. Drop fire down into the brush around the truck."

"You two want me to *light* the ground around the fire engine *on fire?*"

Tara nods. "Yes." She turns and begins yanking hose from the engine, the muscles in her arms bunching with the motion. "You two will light it, I'll douse it. And that's how we make it through this." Tara jerks her chin toward the woods. "The fire's on the forest's edge. If it hits this sage, we're cooked. It'll rush toward us, ten to fourteen miles an hour. So we'll burn wedges at a time before it gets here."

"Like pizza slices, with the engine being that little plastic white circle Domino's puts in the middle," Hank pipes in. "Or is that Papa Johns? Anyway, that'll be the engine. I'll be right beside you, Sparky. Great name for a firefighter, by the way."

"I'm not a firefighter," Sparky says.

"You are today," Tara says as she leans forward and lights the wick of the drip torch. Hank lifts Sparky's T-shirt to cover his nose and slaps his back.

It takes nearly an hour, Sparky and Hank steadily walking the fire away from the engine in triangles, spreading from the truck. The flames gnaw the ground immediately. The heat makes Sparky's jeans feel like hot pads pressed against his legs. The smoke makes his eyes and lungs burn. All around him the air is black and orange, black and orange, but he works without ceasing as they ignite and Tara extinguishes.

Finally they have a space about half the size of a football field circling the fire engine. "Is that enough?" Sparky asks as the sage sizzles, black and orange creeping to the edge of the blackened border.

Hank shrugs. "It's my first wildfire."

"Are you kidding me?" Sparky whimpers. But the ground fire hits the edge of their border and stops. Hits and stops. Hits and stops. Hank takes the hose from Tara, reeling it back onto the engine, and Sparky follows Tara into the engine. With the doors and windows closed, the air is finally breathable.

"What a bad day," Sparky mutters.

Tara gulps water from her thermos and then passes it to Sparky. "Nah," she says. "A bad day is when your partner doesn't make it. This was a good day." Sparky tries not to react at the buried compliment. *Partner.* "The crew Hank was supposed to relieve is now behind us. As soon as this sweeps through, they'll be in. You and Hank will go on to camp. I'll hook up with a CAP rescuer, hitching a ride with them, and head toward Pando."

"To find your son?" Sparky asks.

Tara nods, her jaw clenching.

"Is . . . is he okay?"

She pauses for just a second and then nods. "He will be."

Sparky swallows some water from the second thermos Tara hands him. She stares at Sparky steadily. "Are you going to run when the crew gets here?"

Sparky drinks some more, the water washing away some of the ash and guilt in his throat. He shakes his head.

"You're going to be okay too."

Sparky is spared needing to respond by Hank climbing into the engine with them. The firefighter flips on his radio. As he picks up the receiver, Tara glances at Sparky. "You could do this, you know. Be a firefighter. You're a natural. And doesn't it feel good to be the good guy?"

Sparky rubs his forehead. "I made a lot of mistakes. I'm in big trouble."

Tara nods and then peers out the window to the curtains of black smoke closing in. "Look outside, man. Sometimes everything burns around you *but* you."

Sparky listens as Hank gives their location and condition update to the fire camp supervisors. Then Tara's phone rings, and Sparky recognizes his brother's voice on the other end. Skip doesn't even wait for Tara's hello before talking. "Gerty's okay. She's going to be okay. Hayes saved her. He wanted to keep going. Gerty says he isn't hurt."

"Thank you," Tara says, her voice breaking for just a second. "We had a little bit of trouble—"

"Where are you?"

Tara's mouth quirks into an almost smile. "I'm good. I'm okay. Hank and I, we had some help. Someone who needs to talk to you, actually." She holds out the phone and nods at Sparky. He pauses for a second, then grabs it.

"Brother," he says. Skip breathes his name into the phone, and Sparky realizes Skip already knows he's done something wrong. "I've got to turn myself in."

29

HAYES

I tumble forward, through knee-high prickly brush. The holes in my sneakers snare and rip further. So do my jeans and the skin underneath. I barely feel the sting. I barely feel anything.

This is it. This is the forest that Gerty needed to see to know she'd be okay.

The trunks stretch in front of me, some of them so thin that I could curl my hands around them. She said each one is like a hair on the head of the root system, but I think they're more like fingers, spindly and skeletal. Stark and white, spreading in every direction, like a pocket in heaven split and all these trees fell out.

Gerty said Pando wouldn't look special. She said people could pass right by and not know they were above the heaviest, largest, longest-living being in the world. She said he would look old, like a dying forest.

Gerty was wrong.

It doesn't look old at all. It looks new.

I'm the one who is ancient, who is heavy, who is too big, too much.

"I'm not okay," I tell Gerty. "You were wrong about that, too. I'm here but I'm not okay." Only my mouth won't open, and the words don't come out.

She hears me anyway, because I hear her laugh. I feel her breath against my face as she whispers, "What are you so afraid of?"

No. *No.* Gerty isn't here. She's in a hospital somewhere. She hates me now. Everyone hates me now. "Dying alone," I answer her anyway. When I open my eyes, she's right there in front of me, rolling her eyes at me.

"Everyone dies alone." And then she's gone.

I fall into one of the trees. I slide down it, my back pressed against the bark and my legs sprawled in front of me. Maybe I'm a tree too. Maybe my legs are roots. My hands fall to my sides. My fingers cover roots that dig into the soil around me.

I thought when I got here, I'd have answers. I'd know how to untangle this huge mess I'm in. Know where to go, what to do. But I don't know anything at all. What am I supposed to do now?

I look up, and sunbeams pierce the canopy of leaves. Suddenly the light shifts. The world quakes. Gerty called Pando a trembling giant, and I didn't understand. Now I see. The world shakes as each leaf moves on its own in the breeze, casting coin-sized shadows in all directions. Everything tilts and shifts. All around me I hear the leaves' music as they tremble.

"What are you afraid of?" Gerty asks me again. No, it's Charlie. Maybe it's Pando. "What are you afraid of?"

"Being alone," I answer them all. The leaves dance again, the sound like laughter. And I can't blame them for mocking me, the boy who ran away because he's afraid of being alone. Or laughing because they know I'm lying. I'm not afraid of being alone.

I'm afraid of being *left* alone.

The trees stop moving. The world steadies for a moment. Then another breeze drifts through, and it transforms again. Mom is there, a speck in the distance.

She's running through the woods, her mouth stretched as though calling my name. I can almost hear her, but I know this isn't real. When I close my eyes, she'll be gone. The closer she gets to me, the farther away she'll be. Because this is the dream, isn't it? What I want is so huge, so big, and it'll never stop being a little bit farther away.

I close my eyes.

"I see him! He's here!" Mom says. She's screaming my name. More footsteps through the woods, and people in camouflage uniforms with fluorescent vests run just behind her.

"Hayes! *Hayes!*"

This isn't real. This isn't real.

And then I feel her, the calluses of her hands against my cheeks. "Hayes." When I open my eyes, her arms circle around me. She smells like smoke. "Look at me, Hayes."

There are hands under my legs, under my arms, lifting me. Strangers' voices all around and Mom's whisper in my ear. I see the badge on one of their uniforms. Civil Air Patrol.

"You're going to get through this, Hayes," Mom says. And I know she's real. I see the ash in her hair, feel it fall against my cheek. "You're strong enough for this."

Maybe that's how Pando lived.

He simply got through it.

30

GERTY

A few hours after Mrs. Freid leaves, Nanny Pat's phone rings. I sit up and stare at the side of her face as she listens for a while. "Thank you for letting me know," she says, and then adds, "Of course." She hands me the phone. My palm is slick.

"Gerty?" a deep, feminine voice asks.

I nod, forgetting that the speaker can't see me. I thought it would be Alex. *Focus. Take stock.* Nanny Pat smiles at me. "Yes," I say.

"This is Tara. We have Hayes. He's . . . he's going to be okay." She breathes into the phone, and the sound is wind that trembles through my body. I'm shaking so hard that I press the phone against my cheek.

"He's okay?" I ask.

"He will be," she says. "Dehydrated and weak, but we can fix that. We're on the way to the hospital too, but he'll be staying closer to Fishlake."

"Fishlake?"

"Yeah, that's the other reason I'm calling. He wanted me to tell you he made it to Pando. He was pretty insistent about it, actually."

"Oh," I say. "I'm glad he made it."

"*And* he says to tell you that CAP helped rescue him. Also, that you were right."

"About what?"

Tara laughs. "Everything."

"Please . . . please don't be mad at him. We didn't want any of this to happen. We were supposed to be back before anyone even knew we were gone. Everything just . . ."

"Went sideways," Tara finishes for me. "Yeah, that's also happened to me a time or two in the past. I'm not mad at him. Or you."

"Thank you," I whisper.

"But you're both grounded for life. I know I'm not your mom, but I'm going to go ahead and ground you anyway." She laughs, and that makes me giggle too.

"Please tell him he's my best friend."

Tara sighs. "Thank you, Gerty."

"For what?" I ask.

"For being with him when I couldn't."

Nanny Pat leans over the bed to take the phone from me, blocking my view when the door opens again. She turns and stiffens, and then steps aside.

Alex and Jennifer stand in the doorway. Lilith smiles and reaches toward me from where she's strapped to Jennifer's chest.

For a moment we're all frozen except for the baby. And then Alex's hand rises to bury his face as his shoulders tremble with sobs.

Alex tells me that he's furious with me for lying about the ultralight and for stealing the emergency money. Then he tells me he's proud of me for keeping myself and Hayes alive in the woods.

Jennifer sits close to my bed and brushes my hair with Lilith's comb. "We love you, Gerty. We love you so much."

"I know," I whisper. I don't finish the thought as it unfurls like a new leaf in my head. *But that isn't enough.*

"Our land in Oregon, it's real nice," Alex says. "A pond you can swim in. Trees. Just us for miles and miles."

Jennifer's fingers unlace a knot in my hair. "Or you could stay," she says. "We understand if you'd like to stay."

Alex's jaw clenches, but he nods. "We respect your choice."

Nanny Pat sits in the corner, Lilith sleeping with her head against her shoulder. "What do you want, Gerty?" she asks.

I close my eyes and see Hayes in front of me. I picture Pando's roots. I think about how softly my mom is untangling my hair. "I want to be strong," I hear myself say.

I open my eyes to see Alex's lips quirk. He nods as he slaps his hands on his knees.

I'm not done. "But there are lots of ways to be strong. And I *don't* want to be pulled between you anymore."

I'm going to work to repay the money I stole for my plane. Nanny Pat says she'll get me a job at the local airport. "It'll be convenient for you to get to CAP meetings," she says. "*If* they accept you following this incident." But that's a conversation for another time.

I'm going to live with Nanny Pat during the school year and with Alex and Jennifer in the summer.

We might never shake the shadow of losing Matthew.

But maybe I'm strong enough to grow, even with a scar the shape of my brother inside me.

31

HAYES

A month later

Yellow spreads in front of me like an ocean of flame.

When Pando changes color, he does it all at once. All forty thousand trees turn together. A breeze flickers through. I'm ready for it, but Gerty gasps as the trembling giant quakes.

I think about grabbing her hand, but I push mine into my pocket instead. After all, Chief Skip already made that move. He has Mom's palm pressed against his as they stroll through the woods ahead of us. Charlie is skipping ahead of them. I wander away a little to give Gerty some time alone in Pando.

When I come back a minute later, Gerty is tracing an oval on the trunk of the nearest tree with her good hand. "It looks like an eye," she says.

"Are you going back to school tomorrow?" I ask. She went with her parents, missing a week, to get her stuff and help them settle the new land. And so Alex could try to convince her to stay. It feels odd to be around her now. Like those few days apart were enough for everything that happened to be bigger than us.

"Yeah," she says. Her broken arm is in a bright red cast. "Jaxson is going to be thrilled."

"Ah, he's not so bad. He tried to sit with me at lunch," I tell her.

"What did you do?"

"What do you think? Hid in Mrs. Freid's office."

Gerty laughs. But after a moment she's staring back up at the canopy. Then she sighs and twists so her back is to the trunk. She slides down, a mirror of what I did weeks before. It feels so long ago, like years spanned from that moment to now. I feel in my own hands the ground beneath her palm, the curve of the roots.

I look ahead to where Skip and Mom are walking. I spot a flash of orange to my left. For a second I think it might be a fluffy tail darting between the white trunks.

Gerty is watching me when I turn back, a soft smile on her face. "So you're good? You and your mom?"

"Yeah," I say, not pointing out the maybe fox. "She says we need to keep our toes in the black. It's a firefighting term—"

"I know what it means," she interrupts, and I grin. She throws a stick at me, hitting my shin.

"Mom says it's hard to talk about where things went wrong, that it feels like we're there all over again when we do. But she also says we need to remember that we're in the black. It can't hurt us anymore."

Gerty gazes up at the canopy again. I sit beside her, my back along a different trunk, though the roots are the same. "I like that," she finally says.

"So . . . school tomorrow. And then CAP weekends? Don't they start at the end of the month?" I pick up one of the fallen reddish-yellow leaves, twirling it between my finger and thumb.

Gerty catches my eye. Her hair is nearly the same color as the leaf. I slip it into my pocket. "I'm not going to join CAP. That was Nanny Pat's story. Mine is my own."

"What's your story, Gerty?"

She smiles. "I don't know. Maybe I'll be a park ranger. Figure out ways to keep forests going."

I rub at the back of my neck. It's a habit I picked up from Skip, I guess. "So, um. Do you mind if I do it? Join CAP, I mean."

"Really?"

I nod.

"I think you should go for it. But wait to fly until you have a license."

"Deal," I say. I won't get into another plane anytime soon. But more and more I can remember those first few minutes, when we were soaring.

Gerty leans closer to me, our arms brushing. We can't see the roots below us, where they connect and tie. But above us the leaves tremble. The world shifts.

ACKNOWLEDGMENTS

Gratitude and love to Amika Mota, policy director for the Young Women's Freedom Center. Amika, a former incarcerated firefighter, was a consultant in crafting Tara, as well as Hayes's relationship with her, in *When Giants Burn*. Amika is dedicated to revolutionizing the criminal justice system, including a focus on how to support caretakers after incarceration. For more on the YWFC, please visit www.youngwomenfree.org.

Many thanks to Kari Adams and Kirsten Shaw, who cheered on my twisted contemporary *Hatchet* and Gretel story. Kari's husband, Jonathan, a pilot, suggested Gerty be in CAP. This was the first I had heard of the Civil Air Patrol, but as soon as I began researching, I knew instead of stumbling into the woods, Gerty and Hayes were going to crash into them.

Thank you also to Novalee Dean, who shared her

insight as a young CAP member. "I just wish people knew about it more in general," Novalee told me. "It may sound hard—and it is—but it helps you better your character and yourself as a person."

Much love also to the EAA's Chapter 324 in Simsbury, Connecticut. Members provided insight into how to build an ultralight, crash it, and walk away. Any mistakes in this portrayal are mine alone. Particular thanks go to Vincent Carucci, who is building a Legal Eagle ultralight. When I told Vince that Gerty was building her plane from a kit, he tilted his head and said, "Wouldn't it be even cooler if she Huck Finn–ed it together?" And then he told me how he was doing just that. Gratitude also to the other member who then whispered in my ear, "Maybe Vince didn't mention it, but he's also an engineer, which I'm pretty sure helps." And so Nanny Pat became an engineer.

Thank you also to Rita Black, a fellow writer working on a memoir about her childhood off the grid, for sharing with me how that experience shaped her outlook and sharpened her resiliency.

Following these interviews, I had what I needed to get Gerty and Hayes into the woods, but I didn't know how to get them out. My dear friend Rachelle Harper then told me about her uncle. Von Bross is a former smoke jumper and wildfire containment expert, lives mostly off the grid, loves to build airplanes, and is a survivalist. Von was gracious enough to talk with me for nearly three hours. Von is that smoke jumper with the frozen steak in his leg pocket; he actually did stop a wildfire from consuming him and his truck by keeping a toe in the black, and he knows too well why you should stick to eating ants instead of crickets.

Thank you also to my favorite nurse, Amy Harris, for sharing insight into how to craft Gerty's declining health throughout their journey.

The only thing left was Pando. I had heard about the Trembling Giant nearly a decade earlier, become fascinated by it, and talked about it so often that everyone in my family refers to Pando like a person. But I hadn't yet met this pivotal character in Hayes and Gerty's journey. "Let's fix that," my husband said. Though we were in Fishlake for less than three days, we explored enough of the region to figure out where Hayes and Gerty could've landed and what the fictional town of Rabbit could be like, and, of course, to press our spines against one of Pando's trunks. So much love to you, Jon. Love also to Emma and Ben, whose support is invaluable and constant.

So much love, also, to my brilliant editor, Sophia Jimenez. Sophia's vision is incredible, and it's such an honor to work with her.

Thank you to my wonderful agent and friend, Nicole Resciniti, for championing this book.

Thank you to Atheneum designer Debra Sfetsios-Conover

and cover artist David Dean for the gorgeous design. Much love also to the entire publishing team, including Irene Metaxatos, Kaitlyn San Miguel, Tatyana Rosalia, Erica Stahler, Nicole Moreno, Reka Simonsen, and Justin Chanda.